*To Jim
Warm Regards,
George Garden...*

THE SECOND DEATH
of
TOM PENDER

The Second Death of Tom Pender
A Loganhill Press Book/1991
First Edition

Cover art from a painting by Bill Bugg.

All rights reserved.
Copyright 1991 by George H. Gardiner

No part of this book may be reproduced in any manner without permission in writing from the Loganhill Press, Box 1160, Patagonia, Arizona, 85624

Library of Congress Catalog Card Number: 91-62187
ISBN 0-9629335-1-1

This book is a Loganhill Press/Silver Sage Edition.

Printed in the USA

TABLE OF CONTENTS

		Page
Prologue		1

CHAPTERS

ONE	The Death of Jefferson Buell	3
TWO	The Birth of Buell	5
THREE	Tom Pender	7
FOUR	Henry Powell	12
FIVE	Crimp Madsen, Gunfighter	20
SIX	Frank Applegate	26
SEVEN	West Against the Wind	38
EIGHT	The Making of a Killer	56
NINE	L Troop, D Company	63
TEN	Toward Buell	84
ELEVEN	Angeline	92
TWELVE	The Road to Buell	98
THIRTEEN	Doc Jarka	106
FOURTEEN	The Death Of Will Storms	120
FIFTEEN	The First Death of Tom Pender	129
SIXTEEN	The Second Death of Tom Pender	149
SEVENTEEN	Wooden Guns and Rosebushes	160

"THE SECOND DEATH OF TOM PENDER has to do with the searing secrets buried deep in the souls of five men during the violent days of the West in the 1880's. "Gripping", is the word for this near epic story woven with riveting competence that will hold the reader to the last line."
....Nelson Nye, author of over a hundred westerns and four years frontier fiction columnist and book reviewer for the NEW YORK TIMES.

"THE SECOND DEATH OF TOM PENDER is a fast moving book with surprising twists, tender moments, a sizable helping of humor and pathos, plus an O.K. Corral style shootout that the reader will not soon forget. It will be hard to put aside this book until the final page."
Mel Marshall, author and past president of THE WESTERN WRITERS OF AMERICA.

"...this is a terrific story. You have the makings of a western epic on the order of Larry McMurtry's LONESOME DOVE."
....Josh Frank, Editor,   New Your Publisher.

To Ken Maynard, Buck Jones, Tim McCoy, Hoot Gibson, and Tom Mix, who first showed me wagon trains, painted Indians, and the United States calvary.

Five there were, a bridge and a rose,
And Stars that filled the night.
The years, not caring, rolled steadily on,
Till the rose, the bridge, the five,
                Slowly passed from sight.
                    ....Lod Tremmer

The stillness surrounding the slowly swinging body of Tom Pender was interrupted only by the buzzing of the flies around his face and the sound of a shovel digging in the sandy gravel of the dry creek bed.

Henry cut Tom's body down and carried it the short distance up the canyon to the shallow grave he had dug. He brought Tom's hat from under the bridge and after a momentary study of the young mans twisted features he dropped it over Tom's face and filled in the grave.

The first death and burial of Tom Pender was finished.

****

....Frank raised his eyes to Tom's face and shrank even closer to the wall. "We buried you," he whispered, "We hung you and buried you."

"That you sure did," rasped Tom. "In fact, that's sorta what I'm here to see you about."

PROLOGUE

Aged Bonnie Powell's gladiola-laden funeral was held in the parlor of the Wilkerson farmhouse. She held a bouquet of wilting violets in her hand and wore a cameo at her throat. It was the first funeral I had ever witnessed. The Wilkersons owned the farm next to ours in Logan County, Ohio. The year was 1937

Bonnie had never married; instead, she shared the home of her sister Pauline and her husband, Brad Wilkerson. As a boy, I spent many afternoons playing at the Wilkerson place and whenever company dropped by Bonnie would tell them of her brother Henry in Arizona, then she would read parts of a long letter from him that she had kept for years.

"Henry's sending for me next week," she would tell her listeners. At other times she would pull the worn letter from her apron pocket and say to her sister, "A letter came from Henry today, Pauline. He says they have a new schoolhouse in Buell."

Bonnie was a tiny wisp of a woman in her mid-seventies. One afternoon late in August, they found her dead in her rocking chair on the front porch, her head nodding as if in sleep. Henry's letter lay open on her lap. Forty-five years later, I flew the two thousand miles from Arizona to Ohio and spent weeks searching before I uncovered that letter deep in a box of "Aunt Bonnie's things" in the attic of a nephew. It told me the astonishing story of life in an obscure Arizona mining town and the unusual people who lived it; as written by Henry Powell during the 1880's in the town of Buell, Arizona territory.

Before the first word of the story on the following pages was put on paper, I made a trip by horseback into Cayente Canyon of the Dragoon Mountains in southern Arizona. All signs of the road had long been washed away, but against the wall at the far end of the canyon I found the barely discernible ruins of a small town.

Realizing that over one hundred years had passed, I tried to picture the town as it once had been, but the only thing I found of interest was an enormously large bush heavily laden with red roses near what appeared to be the bulwark of an old bridge. I took Bonnie's letter from my shirt pocket and wondered about the spot where Henry had sat when he wrote it. While I stood daydreaming, a gust of wind snatched the pages from my fingers and scattered them along the ground. I left them where they fell and headed down the canyon, intent on putting on paper a recreation of the incredible story of this ill-fated town as it used to be.

As I reached the mouth of the canyon where it opened onto the desert floor, I heard the silvery ringing of a bell from the area I had just left. I heard it so clearly that I still remember the sound like an echo and I know that some day I'll go back to the ruins of Buell.

Buell was born of tragedy and lived its first few years in violence. It seemed to draw men of ill fortune, the sick, the lonely and the demented. This is the story of that unusual town and the unbelievable sequence of events that occurred in the late summer of 1879. It is also the story of some of the people who came to Buell; the how and the why, and the parts they played in the history of this small settlement in the Arizona Territory.

CHAPTER ONE
The Death of Jefferson Buell

With the slow, relentless pace of all prospectors, Jefferson Buell and his mule Ginger trudged through the canyon with head down, eyes half closed. When they rounded an outcropping of rock, they stopped and Buell gazed up the side of the canyon at a slash of quartz on the reddish-brown earth. He dropped the mule's lead rope, took a pick from her back, and scrambled up to the narrow ledge.

His heart beat faster when he saw the lump of rose quartz embedded in the earth. Less than a foot straight in, the quartz became a solid stem. Laying his pack aside, the old man lowered himself for a closer look and his heart nearly stopped, for only inches away was a vain of gold a foot high and as thick as his wrist.

Almost reverently, he put his fingers on the vein, tracing its slickness from top to bottom. He feasted his eyes for long moments on the yellow metal, unable to believe the sight before him. There was the justification for thirty years of hope and heartbreak, the end and the beginning of a dream ten thousand days and nights old. Finally, with chin trembling and tears of joy in his eyes, he wanted to cry out to the world that he had found the gold just as he always said he would. He had to tell the news to someone, so he stood up and called to Ginger, his mule, "Old girl, we have..."

At that instant, the ledge gave way under his feet and in a few seconds the fulfillment of Jefferson Buell's dream ended. His body dropped like the great weight it was, his head bursting on a boulder at the base of the wall. A thick gold watch flew from his pocket and when it struck the ground the cover snapped open, starting a faint tinkling tune. It played over and over until it ran down and stopped on a last lonesome note. The watch lay above the dead man's head like a miniature tombstone, the lid upright, showing the engraving, Jefferson Buell.

It was October, 1877, and the sting of winter was in the air. Jefferson Buell in his prime, had stood as straight and strong as a Ponderosa pine. His eyes were as black as the beard that grew halfway to his waist. He was a loner, and with his mule Ginger, had walked the weary years away searching for the gold he was sure he would find tomorrow.

About the time Ed Schefelein discovered the hill of silver that was to bring about the creation of Tombstone, Arizona, Jefferson Buell lay dying on the floor of a canyon deep in the Dragoon Mountains. Buell and Schefelein had crossed trails, Schefelein going into the foothills of the Burro Mountains to stumble upon a hill of silver that was to bring him fame and fortune. Buell had crossed to the east, into the crooked Cayente Canyon that slashed deep into the western slopes of the Dragoons, to die at the greatest moment of his life.

First Lieutenant Gerald Dennison, searching with a patrol of United States Cavalry for signs of Nana, the Apache renegade, spotted Ginger and thus came upon the body of Jefferson Buell. Following the ledge a short distance east to where it widened, the soldiers made an excavation into the wall of the canyon and laid the body of the old prospector to rest less that a hundred yards from his vein of gold.
Although the lieutenant instructed the troopers that the gold discovery was to be confined to his official report, hours after they returned to Fort San Carlos the story spread far and fast. In a matter of days, men from all walks of life came pouring into Cayente Canyon. Claims were staked, shanties sprang up, a town was born and they named it Buell.

CHAPTER TWO
The Birth of Buell

Buell, Arizona Territory, was a hell of a place to live and a hell of a place to die. Incredible though it may seem, a young cowpoke by the name of Tom Pender was to die twice in the streets of Buell within a few months.

Buell was a mining town in the Cayente Canyon of the Dragoon Mountains in southern Arizona. Tom had come to Buell more or less by accident, but it was not so with some of the other inhabitants.

Take Frank Applegate, who ran the general store. Frank was a tall, heavy-set man with sun-whitened blond hair. He was a quiet, pleasant man, polite and hardworking, but he was also a coward. He came to Buell with his wife Opal, his daughter Nan and his son Danny. Only he and Opal knew that in years gone by his cowardice had caused the deaths of his father and his eldest son. The tragedies had filled him with a deep sickness which he brought with him to Buell.

It was inside him when he woke in the morning and when he went to bed at night. Frank had come to Buell seeking peace and a new life, but the day was soon to come when he would play a major part in one of the most calamitous events to occur in the Old West, and he, too, would die on the sun-scorched streets of Buell.

Then there was Henry Powell. Henry was a blacksmith, a giant of a man who worked endless hours at his forge and anvil, bare to the waist, his bulging muscles glistening with sweat. Although he was a tobacco-chewing, whiskey-drinking man, he appeared to have the gentleness shown by most men of his enormous size.

But Henry was insane, his sanity having been ripped from him the day he was forced to watch his bride tortured and slaughtered on the plains of Colorado Territory by Yellow Wolf and his band of Paiutes. Henry had stopped at Buell simply because it was the end of a trail he was aimlessly following, running from the nightmare that tormented him. Now he spent his days releasing a little of his bitterness with each blow of his massive hammer as he pounded away at red-hot metal for hours on end. He, too, would play a role in the bizarre events soon to take place in Buell and he, too, would bleed his life away into the thick dust of Buell's main street.

Jed Dunamore owned the only saloon in town, the China Girl, next to Applegate's store. The China Girl was complete with Mexican waitresses, poker tables, a long mahogany bar and a cigarette-burned piano. Jed had no right hand; it had been blown off by a blast from a shotgun while he was trying to save the life of a friend. Jed was that way; lonely, compassionate and intensely loyal.

Such loyalty had cost him his hand, but years later, during the gunfight in Buell, that loyalty halted the trigger finger of a gunslinger for a split second and in the ensuing events Jed's life was spared. Jed's strange brand of friendship for one man brought him to Buell and his friendship for an entirely different breed of man kept him there.

Of all the misfits and odd characters drawn to Buell, one of the most unlikely was Doc Jarka. Doc was a small man who was never seen without a suit coat and vest and seldom without a thin, black cigar clenched in his teeth. He had come from New England, where he had lost his confidence and self-respect in the operating room of the Boston hospital one January morning in 1874. He was drawn west seeking peace for his soul and a simple kind of happiness. He found it in Buell. Doc was present at both the first and second deaths of Tom Pender and he was the only doctor in attendance at the rebirth of the town.

The execution of Tom Pender could only have happened in a lawless town such as Buell, and the tumultuous gun battle spawned by the execution which took place on the town's main street one hot afternoon in June, 1879, was to become the most catastrophic day of death ever to occur in the history of the American West. Unlike the battle of the O.K. Corral in Tombstone, there was no newspaper to exploit the event; it is pieced together and told here pretty much as it must have happened.

CHAPTER THREE
Tom Pender

Tom Pender rode out of Deming, New Mexico, headed for Tubac on the Santa Cruz River in southern Arizona, where he was to sign on with a wildcat outfit for a cattle drive out of Mexico. Tom had a deceptively boyish face, as many a tough learned when the seat of his pants hit the floor of a saloon along the wide trail of Tom's travels. Tom was small of stature among the men of the west, but every ounce of his one hundred and sixty pounds was sinew and muscle, drawn tight around his small frame like strands of rawhide.

Tom's strength began to develop from the time he was nine years old and living on his father's ranch in Utah. He started earning his beans by wrestling calves at branding time and when his father roped and brought to the branding fire the first calf of the day.

"Okay, son," he said, "put 'er down."

Tom leaped at the animal which was much larger than he, intending to "put 'er down" pronto and win the admiration of his father, but although he tugged and pushed and pulled, the calf would not budge. He encircled the calf's neck with his small arms and twisted will all his might. The, with a sudden flip of her head, the calf threw Tom to the ground. He got to his knees and hurled himself at the animal's front legs and the calf went down in a cloud of dust and flailing feet. Tom made the mistake of grabbing for the hind legs and one of the hoofs hit him solidly in the stomach, the other slashing his cheek to the bone. The animal rolled to its feet and stood quivering and bawling, straddling the boy's body.

Tom's father hurried to help. "I'm sorry, Tom, this is a man's job. We'd better get you home and get that cut patched up. Lordy, your Ma will give us both what-for, I'm thinkin'."

Tom looked up with tears of pain and anger stinging his eyes and pushed his father away. "No, no," he said. He rose and approached the animal a little more warily than before and threw himself on the calf's back.

Loring Pender stood back and watched his son fight for the first step toward manhood.

It was a long fight and Tom was not winning. He was caked with blood and dust, his body ached with fatigue, and he was frustrated and filled with the fear of failure as he attacked the kicking, thrashing animal time and again, but to no avail.

Finally, he stopped and studied the situation, then made a decision; he decided to use brains instead of muscles. He stepped to the calf's head and placed the fingers of his right hand in its nostrils, putting his left hand under its chin, and with a quick upward snap, he flipped the calf to the ground. He dropped to his knees across the calf's legs and held its head down with his hands.

Loring Pender grabbed the heated iron with a speed born of years of practice and burned the brand on the flank.

Tom stood up. "Little slow on that one," he said, "but reckon as how I can handle the next one."

"Yeah, I sure reckon as how you can," his father drawled as he climbed back in the saddle.

Tom's mother died the following year and Loring Pender's interest in life and ranching waned after that. The number of cattle dwindled and the ranch became so run down that when his father died a few years later in the fall of '70, Tom sold out to their longtime friend and neighbor, John Watts.

Packing his few possessions in a saddle roll, Tom headed out to taste of life where he would find it. He had no regrets. With the exuberance of the young and equipped with a fun-loving nature, he spent a day or a week in each town, only to be lured by the excitement and freshness of the next one down the road. Tom loved walking his horse down the main street, looking at the stores and nodding to the people as he passed by. He often tied up in front of the emporium and went inside to wander through the various smells; new leather, peppermint, camphor and kerosene. He would buy a handful of crackers and a hunk of sharp cheese and munch on them as he strolled about. Then after buying a sack of licorice drops he would ride off.

When he hit a town on a hot afternoon, Tom enjoyed having a few beers and bantering with the bartender. In other towns, it was his pleasure to sit in on a game of poker. He was a lively player; he thrilled to the turn of a card, whooping with joy when he won and groaning when he lost. Win or lose, though, he could leave the table with no regrets and move on to his next activity with lightheartedness. He could hold his liquor, as most small men can, and he enjoyed sharing a bottle at the bar with a half dozen cowboys while they laughed and sang, lied a little and as the night wore on, cried a little.

A bottle of whiskey can turn two-hour acquaintances into lifetime friends. Tom liked everyone and thought everybody liked him. This assumption set up the circumstances that changed Tom Pender from a fun-loving boy to a serious-minded man with his first taste of hatred. Tom had ridden into Prattville, New Mexico about mid-morning and after looking it over and liking what he saw, he put his horse up at the livery stable and toured the town on foot. He stopped in the general store for his crackers and cheese, his checker-kibitzing and a sack of licorice. Later, he dozed for an hour or two in a rickety old chair in front of the barbershop. He awoke near mid-afternoon and crossed the street to a Mexican restaurant where he ate a large dish of spicy chili beans. That called for beer.

Next door was Dugan's Saloon. Tom went in and was enveloped in the cool sweet smell of beer and booze. He felt revived and spirited after his nap and beans. "Drinks for everybody, bartender," he called.
To his left were two men about his age. "What do you know! A live one!", said the man closest to him.

"Howdy stranger! What's the occasion?" the other remarked.

Throwing out his chest with mock importance, Tom said, "When Tom Pender drinks, everybody drinks." He laughed heartily.

"Is that right?" Tom heard some one say. "And just who the hell is Tom Pender?"

Tom turned and looked into smoky eyes set into an expressionless face that was dirty and bearded. "I'll tell you who Tom Pender is," he said. "He's the hardest-drinking, fastest gun around. He can outdraw, outshoot, outfight, outlove and outlie any man in the Territory!"
The whiskey hit Tom full in the face. It burned his eyes and seeped into his mouth. The black-hatted one replaced the glass on the bar. "He's a fresh kid with a loud mouth and mother's milk still on his chin. That's who Tom Pender is, I'm thinkin'."

Tom reached for the kerchief in his back pocket, but before his hand had moved six inches he was looking squarely down the bore of the stranger's gun. Tom was awed by the incredible speed of the gunman's draw.

One of Tom's new friends elbowed him aside. "Come on, Will, the kid was only spoofing. You're meaner than a tromped on rattler when you're likkered up."

From a scant four feet or less, the blast knocked the cowboy off his feet, his shoulder shattered. The gunman dropped his revolver into the holster and reached for the bottle on the bar.
Before he passed out, the figure on the floor said through clenched teeth, "Will Storms, you whiskey crazy son of a bitch!"

The hand reaching for the bottle stopped in mid-air and with deliberate intent, Will took the few short steps to the side of the fallen man. Tom stood in utter disbelief, for it was obvious that Will intended to kill the helpless cowboy. Tom wore a six-shooter and was pretty good at hitting what he aimed at, but he had no skill in the fast draw. Yet, he had to try to stop the drink-crazed gunman, so he stepped forward, face to face with Will.
"Thinkin' of bein' a hero, kid? Tom Pender, fastest gun in the Territory, you say? I'll give you just three seconds to either draw or drop your gun belt, else I'm going to blow a hole just above your belt buckle."

Fear clutched at Tom's brain for he knew the man meant what he said. Shame and fear lashed him as he ripped loose his gun belt and let it drop to the floor. Will dismissed him with a look of contempt and with slow deliberation drew his gun. Three shots that echoed like one slammed into the body at his feet.

For the first and last time in his life Tom Pender turned and ran. As he escaped from the saloon, the laughter of Will Storms knifed through him and lodged in his brain, where it stayed for a hundred tormented nights. Tom ran to the livery stable and dropped into the corner of an empty box stall with his head between his knees as he trembled in a scalding cauldron of self-contempt.

Crimp Madsen found him there. Crimp ran the livery stable for Henry Ogleby. With the aches and pains of advancing years, he had decided to settle down. In his heyday he had been one of the fastest guns riding the back trails of the New Mexico-Arizona territory, a fact known only to the oldtimers. They remembered that he had once made the notorious Johnny Ringo back down in a saloon in Silver City; but the certainty of one day meeting the younger Will Storms had caused the aging Crimp to hang up his guns.

Crimp now stood beside Tom holding the boy's gun and belt. These had been brought to him with the story of what had taken place in Dugan's Saloon. "I know what's boiling inside you kid and why," he said, "and there's only one way to get it out. You got to learn to handle a gun; to clear leather quicker'n a lizard's tongue. Then you can square things with Will Storms. When you're of mind to start, I'll teach you how it's done." Tom looked up, raising his hand, and Crimp pulled him to his feet. "We'll start tomorrow," he added. "Meanwhile, you bunk here tonight."

Tom was the first customer of the day at White and Eli's Store the following morning, where he bought four boxes of forty-four caliber cartridges. Tom Pender was no longer a boy buying a bag of licorice, he was a man with a mission and he was on his way to learn how to kill a man.

CHAPTER FOUR
Henry Powell

Henry Powell was a man of violence and incredible strength. His uncontrollable temper, coupled with his devastating strength had been the tools of fate that prodded him into moments of destruction, followed by years of remorse.

He arrived in Buell during a downpour. Thunder was a continuous roar until the ground shook and the black clouds spat out bolts of lightning that snapped and cracked at the boulders along the canyon walls. The sound and fury of the storm was a terrifying experience to man and beast, yet through it all walked a giant of a man whom the people of Buell were to know as Henry Powell.

Henry stopped for a moment in front of the China Girl Saloon. If there was anything he liked better than a chew of twist tobacco, it was rye whiskey. Squaring the large canvas bag on his back, he headed for the door.

Henry's back trail wound through half the West, beginning in the town of Walnut Bend, Logan County, Ohio. Until he was sixteen, he had lived on a farm with his mother and three sisters after his father had been killed in a skirmish with the Wyandot Indians. With a hired hand and Henry's help, his mother had continued to run the farm. It was a good farm, with black, loamy soil and corn that grew higher than a man's head. Henry had watched the wind whip golden waves through fifty acres of wheat along the banks of the Mad River.

His father had also put out a fine orchard. There were sweet apples and tangy russets, crisp MacIntosh and Maidenblush, Sheep's Nose and Grimes Golden. Every summer, his mother filled the cellar with jars of fruits, jellies and vegetables. Hams and sides of bacon hung in the smokehouse. Henry had shot many a pheasant and wild turkey on Bristol Ridge and he fished for trout in Mad River, often swimming there on hot summer afternoons.

He was waist-deep in those things that make for comfort and contentment, yet he was restless and full of the dreams of faraway places. Finally, his desire to roam grew so strong that he knew one day soon he must start walking west.

The day came sooner than he anticipated.

Henry quit school in the fourth grade because he was too big to fit behind the desk, so the teacher had given him a kitchen chair along the wall. But, the other children teased him mercilessly and laughed at his size, so one day he walked out of the one-room schoolhouse and never went back.

When he turned sixteen he was a full-grown man whose strength had never been tested. Soon thereafter, however, the people of Walnut Bend got an idea of his tremendous power.

It was the Fourth of July and the town was full of people gathered for the celebration. There were speeches and fireworks, barbecued meat and beer. The town square was alive with boys running nowhere, yelling and shouting with barking dogs close on their heels. The judging of homemade pies and pickles, jams and preserves, cakes and cookies was under way. The horseshoe pitching contest was next and Ty Corbin always won that. Then there was a horse-pulling competition on the vacant lot behind Black and Williams Hardware; Jeff Walgorson and his team of dappled grays had been the winner three years running and was the favorite to win again.

The event that nobody had ever won was the rock-lifting contest held in front of Salzman's Barbershop every year. Along the edge of the sidewalk was a granite boulder approximately four feet high and just the right size for a man to wrap his arms around and clasp his hands. How it got there nobody ever knew, but for years the strong men in the county had been trying to move the "Liftin' Rock", as it was known; no one had ever succeeded. It was a time looked forward to every Fourth of July, when four or five of the strongest men would squat down, each in turn, take a tight grip on the rock and heave with all their might; teeth clenched and blood vessels popping, they could not budge it.

On this day, Henry came to town with his father's old ten-gauge shotgun, intending to compete in the clay pigeon shoot. He had come early to see the sights and perhaps buy a sack of Maude Worthington's taffy candy or a big slice of watermelon. He wandered into the crowd in front of the barbershop, then stood and watched as "Squirrel" Kennedy tugged and struggled with the granite boulder and finally gave up.

The men laughed, shook their heads and muttered to each other. Ed Arbogast was standing on the sidewalk looking across at Henry. "Henry," he called, "why don't you give it a try?"

Henry stepped back and started to turn away, but the men closed around him, urging him on. He was pushed forward until he was standing in front of the boulder and calls of encouragement came from the crowd. "C'mon, Henry, you can do it!"

"Give it a try, kid!"

"Show these fellas what a real man is!"

"Pick 'er up, Henry, and the soda pop's on me!" Squirrel Kennedy called.

Henry felt trapped, but he looked the boulder over carefully and decided to take his turn at it. Planting his feet on each side of the boulder, he stooped down and wrapped his arms firmly around it. Slowly, he began to lift and the long, thick muscles in his back bulged from the strain. He heaved with every ounce of strength in his mighty body until the blackness in front of his tightly-closed eyes turned red and his face was drenched with sweat. Sharp jabs of pain stabbed through his body and the cords on his thick neck stood out like bars of steel. His body began to tremble as he lifted with all his might, but the boulder would not move.

Henry gave up. He began to relax, to let his knotted muscles slowly return to normal. And as he stood up he heard the sound of mocking laughter, the sound he had heard so often in childhood. It burned and tormented his brain until the blood began pounding at his temples, carrying a new surge of strength throughout his giant frame. he squatted before the boulder again and the laughter began to die out. Slowly, he straightened to a standing position and in his powerful arms he held the massive piece of granite. The laughter was stilled.

Henry swung to his right and took a step, then, carefully, another, until he finally lowered his burden ten feet from its original resting spot. Without a word to anyone, he walked through the path opened for him, crossed the square and headed for the farm. It was his last trip to Walnut Bend. The group of silent men who watched him go would tell and retell a hundred times about the day they saw Henry Powell lift the "Liftin' Rock".

Everything about Bonnie Powell was little, except her enthusiasm for life. She was the energetic member of the Powell family. No one could get as excited about finding a baby rabbit, the first flower of spring or Christmas morning as Bonnie. She cried when her pet calf was sold and laughed with glee when baby chicks were hatched. It was her tiny hands that tended the flowerbeds and later filled the house with vases of blossoms. Bonnie's usual way of getting somewhere was to run; to the spring house, to the meadow or to the mailbox, her golden hair streaming in the wind and her blue eyes filled with the joy of living.

Bonnie had just passed her fifteenth birthday and on this Independence Day, she was excited at the prospect of a day in town. Her pony, Prince, was tied and waiting for her at the front gate. Her sisters, Rachel and Pauline, had gone ahead with their mother when the Williams's had stopped by on their way to town. She was tying her hair back when she heard footsteps on the porch. The screen door opened and Pete, the hired hand, entered the room. His work clothes were dirty and sweat-stained, he was unshaven and bleary-eyed and unsteady on his feet. He obviously had been drinking; Pete never came into the house except at mealtime, so Bonnie was puzzled.

"What is it you want, Pete?" she queried.

Pete leered through whiskey-reddened eyes. "I want you, sweetie," he said and started toward her.

Henry was a half mile up the road when the first scream reached his ears, but he was so lost in thought that it was not until the second one that he realized the screams were coming from his home. He broke into a run and on reaching the side fence, vaulted it and burst through the kitchen door. The sight that met his eyes filled him with rage. He reached down and grabbed Pete in a crushing grip, raising the man in the air and brought him sharply down across his knee; Pete's back snapped like a stick of wood and he screamed in agony as he slipped to the floor.

The sight of Bonnie's crumpled body and her moans intensified Henry's rage. Almost weeping in his fury, he stomped the man's head and body as he would a rat. He stopped only when he saw Bonnie trying to struggle to her feet. Henry picked her up in his arms and turned to look back at the figure on the floor. He knew Pete was dead and it filled him with satisfaction.

He carried Bonnie outdoors and sat down under the giant elm tree in the yard. There, he cradled his tiny sister and gently rocked her back and forth as he would a baby. That is where his mother and sisters found them later in the day.

Doc Davis was summoned and after examining her he assured the family that Bonnie had not been injured. The terror of the incident would probably never completely leave her mind, Doc said, but it would greatly diminish as she grew into womanhood.

Henry told his story to old Doc. "Henry, this must be reported to the sheriff," Doc advised. "There will be an inquest and probably a trial, but under the circumstances I'm sure you have nothing to worry about."

They were in the hall outside Bonnie's bedroom. Henry listened to the doctor's words then started down the stairs with Doc following. Pete's body still lay on the kitchen floor and without hesitating, Henry grabbed the man's feet and started dragging him toward the door.

"Just a minute," said Doc, "I'll give you a hand."

But Henry continued through the door, dragging Pete behind him. Across the yard and through the gate they went with the doctor following behind, trying to get a grip on Pete's shoulders.

"Leave it alone!" Henry said in a voice that commanded obedience. They stopped at the rear of Doc's buckboard and Henry flung the body into the wagon bed as if he were handling a side of beef.

"Get this trash out of here," he said, "afore I feed it to the hogs. And tell the sheriff I'll leave a writin' of what happened. I'm obliged for you takin' care of Bonnie. I'll be leavin' come mornin', but Ma will have your pay next time you come back. Now, I reckon I got things to do." He headed back toward the house and as he reached the porch he called out, "Night, Doc."

"Henry!" Doc shouted, but he received no response. He climbed into the buckboard and picked up the reins. "That boy's right set in his ways," he said to Jinny, his old mare.

Henry went directly to his room at the back of the house. He took a piece of canvas, obtained in anticipation of this day, placed it across the bed and began to pile his personal belongings on it. When he finished, he rolled it tightly and tied it with rope. Remembering then, he went to the bottom drawer of the bureau and took the mouth organ his father had given him, unrolled the canvas and put it among his other belongings, then rolled it up again and tied it. He took the roll downstairs and placed it with his rifle by the front door. Finally, he lit a lamp and sat at the dining room table to write a letter to the sheriff:

Dear Sherif, I kild a varmint today. I don't rightly know what kind it was but Doc Davis can show you. If there's any bounty or reward you can keep it and obliged. Henry Powell.

Henry then wrote a letter to his mother, advising her to sell the farm and move into town with the girls. He told her he was going to California or Oregon, that he would write to her, and that some day he would sent for them all.

He left the letter to the sheriff open on the table, then folded the other and put it under the lamp. When he looked into Bonnie's room she was asleep from the effects of the medicine Doc had given her and his mother had fallen asleep in the big chair by the bed. He walked quietly to the nightstand and turned down the lamp, then headed for his own room and bed.

Long before the sun had risen, Henry was up and

dressed. Even so, he heard his mother in the kitchen, busy with breakfast. He stopped by Bonnie's room but did not awaken her. He did not intend to tell her he was leaving, nor did he expect to see his two other sisters, so he and his mother ate breakfast alone, mostly in silence. When he finished his biscuits and gravy and ham and eggs, he looked up at his mother. "Ma..." he began.

"Henry..." his mother said at the same instant. Henry lowered his eyes and his mother smiled sympathetically. "Henry, I know what you've a mind to do and I know there's no sense in me trying to talk you out of it. I've felt it coming for quite a spell. In the light of what's happened, I reckon it's best you do what you have to do. Your Pa was like that, except that you've got a restlessness in you he didn't have. So, maybe you'll find the thing that's been pullin' at you. If your Pa were here he'd tell you this: If you never do anything you'd be ashamed for us to hear about, you'll be all right."

Henry stood up. "I'll be gettin' at the chores," he said.

Sunlight was streaming across the eastern sky when he returned to the house. Picking up a couple of biscuits as he passed the kitchen table, he put them in his jacket pocket and went through the house looking for his mother. He happened to glance through the window on the side of the house and saw her kneeling on a slope a hundred yards distant.

I might've known, he thought, for it was on that slope near the apple orchard that his father was buried. Picking up his roll and gun, he made his way to his mother's side.

Dew on the thick grass sparkled in the morning sunrise and the gentlest breezes carried the smell of hay and the animals in the barn, mixing with the fragrance of the lilacs and roses that grew around the house. Across the way in the timber on Briston Ridge, a flock of crows helped to wake up the world. It all formed a memory that Henry would take away with him.

His mother neither moved nor looked up. Henry placed a hand on her shoulder and bent to kiss her on the cheek. "Bye, Ma," he whispered and walked away. He looked back only once.

When he topped Hatcher's Hill, the place where he had spent the first sixteen years of his life thoughts tugged at him to reconsider. He was at the rail fence that separated the Powell and Hatcher farms. He leaned against the rails to take in the scene in the valley below.

    He gazed at the clump of willow trees at the bend in Mad River where he had played as a boy; at the broad square of wheat, light green now but soon to turn gold; at the field behind the barn with its straight rows of corn, waist high and growing. He looked at the barn, large and comforting, with its ever-present row of pigeons on the ridge. The cattle were grazing in the pasture and the horses were lined along the fence.

    He looked at the house last. It was a big house, painted white with gables trimmed in green. It was stately, proud and protective, filled with love and laughter, reluctant to give up its own. Henry looked at the small window toward the back of the house, the window in his room from which he had looked so many times with longing and wonder at the land to the west. It was toward this land that he now turned to start the long journey that would finally lead him to the town of Buell, Arizona Territory.

CHAPTER FIVE
Crimp Madsen, Gunfighter

Crimp Madsen was gunwise. Long ago he had studied the fast draw and had mastered it. Until age overtook him, there never was a man who could match his speed, which made him the rare case of a gunfighter destined to die in bed.

Tom placed the ammunition on a nail tie inside the livery stable door and, as Crimp walked up, he said, "Let's get at it."

"Hold your horses, boy, we've got a little talking to do first. Lemme see that shootin' iron of yours."

Tom handed his gun to Crimp, butt first. There was a small explosion on the side of his jaw and the seat of Tom's pants hit the dirt floor.

"That's lesson number one, son; don't never, at no time, ever hand your gun to another man. You might as well get it between your ears right off, this is no game we're playin'. If you're gonna wear that hunk of iron, you damn well better learn how to use it."

Tom got to his feet, retrieved his gun and pointed it just above Crimp's beltbuckle. Deliberately, he thumbed back the double-action hammer and two metallic clicks sounded ominously between them. Time stood still for a few moments, then in a voice slightly above a whisper Tom said, "Crimp, you ever do that again, you'll be on your way to boot hill."

The semblance of a smile appeared on a face that had almost forgotten how. "Damnation! I reckon you might make a gunhand after all," he said.

Tom's gun was swept aside with a lightning-fast movement and again the rocklike fist landed on his jaw. The gun went flying and again Tom was flat on his back. Standing over him, Crimp said, "Lesson number two. Don't ever point a gun at a man unless you intend to kill him." He picked up the gun and shoved it in his belt, in case Tom was moved to carry out his threat.

Tom raised himself to one elbow and rubbed his twice-battered jaw. "Might be we'd better call it a day,

Crimp. I don't think I can take lesson number three." Then he smiled and the bond of understanding between man and boy was welded.

"Hell's fire, boy, I just taught you two things in the best way I know that'll likely save your life some day. Now let's get down to how we're gonna milk this cow. Step over to that there barrel while I have a look at how you're hung together." Crimp took a halter rope and placed the end of it on the barrel. "Now, with your right hand show me how hard and how fast you can slap the end of this rope. Spread your feet a little, stand loose and get ready at the count of three."

At the count Tom slapped, Crimp jerked the rope, and all Tom succeeded in doing was to sting his palm. Crimp replaced the rope. "Now try it with your left."

Again on the count of three, Tom slapped and Crimp jerked, but this time Tom pinned the rope to the barrel head.

"Well, howdy Hannah! With speed like that and me learnin' you, you'll be another Pore Laidlaw--Pore was the fastest left hand draw I ever knew.

"Howsomever, right now you got some errands to do. First, take this gun o' yourn over to Jake the blacksmith and have him grind off the front sight. Then have the holster moved to the right side of your gunbelt and fastened so the gun butt points forward. You're gonna learn the cross draw, kid, just like I did. It's the most natural move for the arm muscles; there's no backward or unnatural raisin' and lowerin' of the arm with the cross draw. And while you're at the store, get a quart Mason jar."

"What the hell do you want with a Mason jar?" Tom asked.

"Well, boy, you're gonna build a little speed. I reckon there's ten thousand flies in this stable and when you get back here you're gonna sit on that barrel, and usin' your left hand only, you're gonna catch one hundred flies in mid-air and put 'em in that Mason jar. When you get that done, I'll feed ya. That's lesson number three."

Later that afternoon Tom stood in the door of the livery stable and watched as a wagon passed carrying the body of the murdered cowboy in a pine box, heading for the cemetery on a nearby hill. Again, the feeling of shame and the utter senselessness of the encounter swept over him. Moments later, the sensation was replaced with anger-tinged hatred when he looked up the street in the opposite direction and watched Will Storms mount his horse and ride out of town. Two men moving in opposite directions, one dead and one soon to be; at least that was the way Tom planned it.

Tom extracted a cartridge from his pocket and with the small blade of his pocket knife he patiently proceeded to scratch letters into the casing. Crimp came up behind him just as he finished and saw the bright lines in the brass that spelled out WILL STORMS. There was no comment from Crimp as Tom dropped the cartridge into his shirt pocket to await another day.

Tom sat, sweated, and grabbed at flies. The heat and the dust and the damnable insects were fraying his nerves until Crimp broke up the monotonous practice one afternoon when he walked into the livery stable carrying a gunny sack. He upended it and gave it a shake and a writhing rattler dropped to the floor. In answer to Tom's quizzical look, Crimp said, "You're gonna learn from this critter."

The snake was coiled into a tight circle. Crimp took a hay fork and bade Tom squat down beside him. "When this feller strikes, I want you to watch and learn. Just before he strikes you'll see his head draw back a mite. That means he's bunchin' his muscles and locking them. When he decides to strike it's just a matter of him pulling the trigger, the rest is reflex action. That's what you're gonna learn to do with the muscles of your arm. When you decide to draw, the only work your brain needs to do is set the muscles an' lock 'em. Then, when you're ready to make your move, the brain releases the muscles and the rest is as fast as this rattler."
With that, Crimp shoved the fork handle forward and, faster than Tom's eyes could follow, the snake's fangs struck the wood then it drew back to its original position.

"The only difference is," Crimp continued, "nature gave this old boy the ability to move like lightning.

You've got to develop it. You got to train your brain and the muscles of your left arm to work just like I explained it."

Crimp took a plug of tobacco from his pocket and tossed it toward the snake's head. "Now," he said, "we got another little test to see if you have the makin's of a gunhand. When Mister Snake hit the fork handle I measured the length of his strike. That plug of tobacco is layin' just at the edge of his range. Usin' your left hand, I want you to beat him to it."

"Whoa-ho!" Tom exclaimed. "You're crazy as hell!"

"Listen boy, after you've earned a rep you're gonna come up against some jaspers a helluva lot meaner'n this rattler and damn near as fast. They'll set out to blow your shirt buttons right past your backbone. Now, it makes no nevermind how fast you may be, if you ain't got that extra ounce of guts, your first gunfight will be your last and I reckon we might as well find it out right now. In the first place, I'm not askin' you to grab the tobacco, just knock it aside. You got the advantage 'cause you're gonna move first.

"Remember, Mister Snake needs a fraction of a second to draw back his head and lock his muscles before he strikes. Why, hell, I bet he'll miss you by a full inch! You can beat him; the big question is, do you have the guts to try? If you don't, my advice is, give your gun away and take up store clerkin' or barberin' or such. That's the way the saddle fits; it's up to you."

Tom weighed Crimp's words and found they hung square on the hook. He looked across at the snake and its eyes appeared to be staring directly into his, its flicking tongue indicating it was ready whenever he was. In those few mesmerizing moments, with hot sweat on his face and ice water in his stomach, Tom had the feeling that the snake had heard the conversation and was planning a diabolical move to bury its venomous fangs into the back of his hand.

That's crazy, he thought, and so, with all the speed he could muster, he swiped at the square of tobacco. The rattler struck and the plug of tobacco flew across the floor.

Tom jerked his hand in front of his eyes and looked for fang marks but found none. The snake had missed.

Tom looked over at Crimp. "You fleabitten, broken down bastard! Some day I'm gonna cut your ear off and make you eat it!"

Crimp picked up the plug of tobacco, bit off a corner and, with his peculiar smile, proffered the rest to his young friend. "Chaw?" he offered, nonchalantly.

Tom's mouth was like cotton as he headed for the water bucket. When he returned, Crimp had taken a bull whip from the wall and was standing about four paces from the rattler.

"Now I'll show you what three years as a mule skinner can do," he said. With a flick of his arm he sent the string of rawhide whistling through the air. There was a crack like a gunshot and the rattler's head sailed across the room. Then he coiled the whip and hung it on a nail. "Close your mouth, son, a sparrow might fly in," he said to Tom as he walked past.

Crimp's left foot made a half-twist each time he put it down, so he looked like a man walking through mud. His slouched shoulders and great bulk made him a man not easily forgotten. Tom stared at his back as he walked away and new admiration for the man welled up within him. A man to ride the river with, he mused. A fly buzzed by as he watched Crimp. "You can go to hell," he said to it. "I'm playin' with rattlers now!"

Tom had taken to sleeping on the roof of the room behind the livery stable. He liked the coolness of the night, the soothing sound of the wind in the eucalyptus trees and the occasional call of a wandering coyote. But most of all he liked the aloneness.

One night after beans and bacon and a little conversation with Crimp, he climbed the ladder to the roof. Suddenly he felt melancholy and lonely. He stretched out on his roll and his mind flew back to the ranch where he had grown up. He smelled his mother's cooking in the big kitchen, felt his father's hand on his head and saw his smile. He remembered the scary nights when he and his mother were alone while his father made the long trip to town for supplies, and he recalled the relief when his dad returned home. He smiled as he thought of the ruckus his mother raised when she found out he'd been keeping a half-grown raccoon in the loft where he slept.

He'd guess the greatest excitement they had ever had was the day his father pulled the big surprise on his mother. It started when his father announced he had to make a special trip to town.

"We're not needin' anything," his mother said.

"I'm goin' in for a four-legged critter. Somethin' special," his father answered.

Late afternoon of the third day, his father had driven the team through the gate, but instead of turning toward the barn he drove to the house and stopped at the front door. On the back of the wagon was something large, covered with canvas. His father had called to his mother, then told her to close her eyes. He led her to the side of the wagon, threw aside the canvas and told her to look.

There on the wagon bed, with all its glistening glory reflecting the rays of the evening sun, stood a baby grand piano. He remembered the cry of joy from his mother, the smile and tears and the big hug for his father. Many winter nights thereafter he heard his mother play, sometimes with neighbors around and sometimes just for him and his father; there was special music on Sunday evenings and at Christmas and Easter. In later years as he was riding in off the range, he could hear the piano from afar and the sound remained in his memory.

The last time the keys were touched was by the minister's wife at his mother's funeral. Afterward, his father closed and locked the piano and dropped the key into his pocket.

Tom's daydreaming turned to night dreaming and again he wrestled a calf by the branding fire.

CHAPTER SIX
Frank Applegate

Mattie Applegate was alone in the back room of the stage station. The fire in the corner fireplace sent out fingers of light and shadows danced across the ceiling as she lay in bed in a corner of the room awaiting the birth of her second child. The wind shrieked outside the log building and the temperature stood at thirty below zero.

The stage station in Ely, Nevada had been home for Mattie and her husband Jeremiah for almost a year. They had met and married in California, where Mattie lost her first child at birth. Jeremiah worked for the Overland Stage Company and had been sent to Nevada to establish a stage station on the North Fork River. Although life was rugged in the vast wilderness, Mattie was happy working side by side with her husband.

During their first spring, she planted a garden and a flower bed with seeds brought from Califronia. They lived in a sod shanty while the station was being built and Mattie did her cooking and baking outdoors. Each evening, she watched with awe as the sun went down behind the towering Independence Mountains. What other woman has a thousand-acre valley for a kitchen, she thought.

Jeremiah loved what he was doing and he loved Mattie and her exuberance for living. He left one morning to extend the trail he was laying out to the east and when he returned, he brought a small flock of twelve or fifteen sheep and half a dozen lambs. The flock became Mattie's pride and joy. She talked to the animals as if they were people. Whenever Jeremiah butchered one of her flock Mattie was inconsolable for days, but in time her gay spirit would return and she bubbled with vitality until the next occurrence.

The stage station was completed in mid-summer and Mattie and Jeremiah moved into their room at the back. Mattie never liked their new quarters; the room was dark and the damp air smelled musty. Jeremiah spent the early fall building a corral that would hold two dozen or so stage horses. He was able to hire some peaceful Paiute Indians from a small village up on the North Fork to help him and an Indian squaw to help Mattie now that the baby was coming. Neither he nor Mattie could pronounce her Indian name, so they called her Mouse because she made little squeaking sounds as she worked.

It had been a fairly mild winter. Christmas had come and gone and there had been very little snow. Although the nights were cold, the days were clear and mild. So, with the baby not expected for almost a month and with Mouse to keep Mattie company, Jeremiah decided to go to Fort Shelbourne, some forty miles to the south. They needed supplies and he wanted to mail a report to the office in California. He figured he would only be gone four or five days, so after laying in a supply of firewood and filling the water barrel, he kissed Mattie goodbye and rode off.

On the morning of the third day, Mattie felt a strangeness in the air almost from the time she got up. First, Mouse did not show up, and Jeremiah had specifically instructed her to be there early every morning. The Indian village was less than a mile away, so Mattie walked to the front door of the station to see if she could spot Mouse coming. Then she noticed that the sun was not its usual golden yellow, but very pale, almost white. The air was still and the early morning singing of birds was missing. An unexplainable shiver ran down her back. In the distance she could see a large, gray-black cloud forming over the mountain. She also noticed how unusually warm it was for early December.

Mattie brewed a cup of tea and sat down to contemplate her activities for the day. I'll make a cider cake, she decided. It was Jeremiah's favorite and it would have time to age before he returned.

First, she busied herself with sweeping, dusting, making the bed, replacing the candle stubs with new ones, and filling the iron kettle by the fireplace with water from the barrel in the corner. She rested in a rocking chair long enough to finish a blanket she had been knitting for the baby, then she laid out the utensils and ingredients for the cake. Suddenly she felt chilly.

That's strange, she thought. It had seemed warm outside earlier, but now she tossed a log on the fire and returned to her baking. All at once, there was a strong gust of wind and a puff of smoke belched out of the fireplace, drifting across the room. Looking out the window, she noticed it was getting dark.

At that instant, the first sharp stab of pain struck her lower abdomen. It left her body and coursed upward to her mind, where it reappeared as fear. Mattie cupped her stomach with her hands and whispered to the empty room, "Oh my god, the baby is coming!"

Another strong gust of wind rattled the windows. The room was now almost dark. Mattie lit a candle and thought, I've got to get Mouse. She threw a shawl around her shoulders and hurried outside. A blast of cold wind almost swept her off her feet and snow began falling. In a very short time, winter had moved back into the valley. The top half of the mountains had disappeared in the clouds and the valley was white with the approaching storm. The teepees of the Indian village would very quickly be swallowed up in the coming snowstorm, so a trip there was out of the question. Mattie went back inside and closed the door.

If Mattie had been at the Indian village early that morning and could have understood Paiute, she would have heard Wahoka, Mouse's husband, order his wife not to visit the home of the white eyes that day.

"A bad storm is coming. There will be much snow and cold. The white woman has enough food and wood; she has no need of you. You are needed here. You can return when the storm is gone, one, maybe two days. I will eat now, and sleep until the storm goes away."

Obediently, Mouse picked up a piece of firewood and brained a dog sleeping in the teepee. She began to skin it in preparation for the boiling pot, squeaking softly as she worked.

Meanwhile, Mattie sat on the edge of the bed to gather her wits. She knew she should not panic and she also knew that she could not expect Mouse's help, nor would Jeremiah be back in time. She began to talk to her self.

"Well, Mattie Applegate, you aren't the only woman ever to have a baby alone. This is not your first, so you know what to expect. You must get things ready and above all, don't go to pieces."

Her own voice calmed her down and she set about building up the fire. As she hung blankets across the window and door against the wind, she felt her second labor pain. After a moment she swung the iron kettle into the fireplace, put a dipper nearby and moved the wooden tub to the side of the bed. She got the baby's things, as well as scissors, iodine, thread and beeswax, mentally checking off each item as she went. Then, because she could think of nothing else to do, she undressed, put on her flannel nightgown and crawled beneath the quilts. She glanced at the calendar above the bed and saw that it was December 31. Outside, the storm raged in full fury. snow was piling up rapidly and the temperature was well below zero and falling fast. Mattie felt another pain and held her breath until it was over.

For a while she passed the time thinking of some of the enjoyable things she and Jeremiah had done last summer. She even dozed once or twice. Then, as the pains came closer together, she rehearsed what she must do when the baby was born. Twice she got out of bed to build up the fire and knew the second time that before she did it again the baby would be born.

As the birth came closer and the pains became more severe, she was surprised to find that the fear had left her, replaced by the peace of anticipation that left her calm and confident. All she had to endure was the pain and any woman could do that.

Either the baby was coming early, or she had miscalculated. Wouldn't Jeremiah be surprised to come home and discover he was a father! Mattie had tried to be brave during the birth of their first child, what with the doctor and a neighbor at her bedside, but she realized now that she could cry aloud if she wanted for there was no one to hear. She remembered the doctor's instructions from years ago about bearing down with the contractions, so she did what she had to do and screamed into the darkness.

Mattie had a difficult, agonizing time of it. The pain tore through her like a living thing and, at the moment of birth, her long, piercing scream blended with the shrieking of the storm.

She fought to remain conscious and with a knowledge inherent to all women, she performed the necessary duties. She lifted the child and spanked it into its first breath, then tied and cut the cord. In a few minutes she had taken care of herself and the baby and had it bundled in a blanket and lying at her side.

It was a boy and she thought he already looked like Jeremiah. She was happy and proud and only mildly concerned that she was still bleeding. It would stop shortly, she was sure.

But it didn't. Mother and baby slept and the storm outside began to abate. When morning came and Mattie awoke, the bed was soaked with blood. She was weak and very drowsy, but she was aware of the seriousness of the situation. However, she couldn't arouse herself to do anything about it, even had she know what to do. The baby slept on and as Mattie looked at her tiny child she smiled away her fears.

By noon the storm was over and the sun was out. Mouse trudged across the whiteness and found the house bitter cold and Mattie too weak to rise, but Mattie managed to instruct Mouse to bring her sewing box. Feebly, she dug through it and found a pencil and a scrap of paper. She wrote a few words, and as the last tiny flame in the fireplace went out she closed her eyes.

When Mouse gave the paper to Jeremiah two days later, it read:

Franklin Pelham Applegate.

Squirrel Woman was the wife of Brown Eagle, chief of the Northern Paiutes, and mother of White Wind, who was born two days before the great storm. Mouse brought Jeremiah's son to the teepee of Squirrel Woman and he nursed at one brown breast while the tiny son of the Paiute chief fed at the other. Because his hair was red, the white boy became know as Little Fox among the Indians. His near-twin, White Wind, would one day wear the robes of his father, Brown Eagle, and songs would be sung in many Paiute lodges about his bravery, while Little Fox would struggle with cowardice until, as Frank Applegate, he would die on the streets of Buell, Arizona.

Lame Bull, a lesser chief and leader of the Paiutes, occasionally took his people through the mountains beyond the Green River Valley to hunt. At night their teepees and campfires could be seen on the banks of the North Fork, and the next morning they would be gone without leaving a sign until about thirty of forty days later when their camp would magically reappear.

Mouse continued as housekeeper for Jeremiah and in time she brought Little Fox to visit his father. While the child was an infant Jeremiah never asked to hold him, and when the boy was old enough to walk he was totally ignored by his father. Sometimes, Jeremiah would stare at his son for long periods. The, without a change of expression, he would turn and walk away.

The Ely Station became a regular stop on the Overland Stage Route and two or three years later, the Pony Express was added. Because Ely was mid-point, Jeremiah often saw the express rider from the west leap from his winded pony and, with his mail pouch over his shoulder, run for his already-moving replacement; and before he hit the saddle, the westbound rider would be sliding his horse to a stop.

Frank now spent the nights in the Indian village and the days at the station with his father. He was frightened of the tall man who stared at him so strangely, but wherever Jeremiah went Frank was close by, peeking from under a gate or behind a post. Very little went on that Frank did not watch in wonder.

During the heavy snows and bitter cold of the winter the boy stayed with Mouse for days at a time. Just before winter set in the horses had been moved to the low country and a stage travel switched to the Southern routes. During the monotony of winter, Jeremiah spent long days and endless nights pacing the floor and longing for his beloved Mattie.

In the spring of 1858, when the boy was five years old, a small incident took place that decided the question of whether he would grow up as an Indian or a white man. It was mid-afternoon on a warm April day and Jeremiah was replacing the fence post in a corral. He sensed Frank's presence before he saw him and when he turned he saw that the boy held something in his hands. He squatted down beside his son and Frank handed him a baby rabbit. The boy's eyes searched his father's face for a few seconds, then he turned and ran for the house as fast as his little legs would carry him. Jeremiah's heart was warmed.

That night the three of them shared the bedroom; Jeremiah, his son and the baby rabbit. The next morning the Indian village had disappeared. The Paiutes had moved into the rugged hunting grounds, but this time without Little Fox.

Jeremiah began to enjoy his son and life started to move again. He looked past the ragged mountains into the long line of tomorrows and started to plan.

One day they rode to Fort Shelbourne, Frank on the saddle in front of his father. Jeremiah wired his resignation to California and requested a replacement. As he and Frank rode home he felt the return of a familiar happiness he had known a few years ago.

On the morning of July 13, 1858, Jeremiah loaded most of their belongings on the westbound stage for Carson City. Then, taking Frank by the hand, he walked to a knoll by the river. Knee-deep in mountain daisies, they stood hand in hand for a while at Mattie's grave. As they rode away, Jeremiah noticed that the Paiute village had returned to the banks of the North Fork. The cycle of Indian life continued, following the patterns their ancestors had worn into the trails of time.

The white man and his son left the valley of the North Fork to seek a new and better way to live. Therein lay the reason why one day the red man would give way to the white invader.

Jeremiah made a home for his son in Carson City, Nevada. He tried his hand at a number of jobs and finally hired on as a deputy marshal. He liked the job, making friends easily, and quickly earned a reputation as a good lawman. Then, soon after he started his third year on the job, Marshal Denton was brought back to town lying across his saddle. He had been dry-gulched among the rocks of the high country while trailing a fugitive and the town was left without a marshal. The aldermen promptly voted Jeremiah into the office.

He was wearing the marshal's badge a dozen years later when he was murdered in the streets of Carson City on the eve of his son's wedding.

Frank had grown into a tall, handsome young man with a pleasant manner and a delightful way of squinting his eyes when he turned on the full effect of his smile. The red hair of his childhood had turned blond and he made a striking figure astride his Appaloosa. The young ladies in town sent invitational glances his way, but the girl who won his heart was the parson's daughter, demure, black-eyed Opal Hetherington.

That Frank had made her his choice soon became evident to everyone. Opal became his constant partner at the square dances on Saturday nights and Frank was consistently the high bidder for her box supper at the church socials. When the announcement of their betrothal appeared in the Carson City Examiner, it surprised no one but Jeremiah. Like many fathers, he had not noticed what was going on under his nose, or if he had, he had not taken it seriously.

In keeping with Opal's sentimental nature, she chose January first for her wedding day, thus creating a future cause for a triple celebration; New Year's Day, their anniversary and Frank's birthday. "Three new beginnings!" she told Frank delightedly as they made their plans.

"Yes," said Frank with a grin, "and also three endings."

The night before the wedding, with the help of some young friends, Frank and Opal were decorating the church. It was New Year's Eve and the night was cold and dark except for the brilliance of countless stars. Opal made Frank leave at the stroke of midnight, following the old belief that the groom should not see his bride on their wedding day until they met at the altar. As the church bell rang in the new year, Frank kissed Opal and whispered, "Happy New Year, darling," and left.

He stopped by the marshall's office. "Happy New Year, Pa," he greeted.

"Happy New Year, son."

"Things seem to be pretty quiet in the old town for New Year's Eve," Frank remarked.

"The celebrating is mostly over and I guess folks are home in bed," his father answered. "Had a little trouble earlier in the evening, though."

"What happened?"

"Oh, Jim and Jesse Kreel are in town and they got a little drunk and started shooting up the Nugget. Jim got a little mean so I had to put a knot on his head and throw him in a cell. Jesse showed up complaining so I ordered 'em both out of town."

"You watch yourself, Pa. Those two are a couple of coyotes at their best. When they're drinkin' they're downright poison."

"I judge we've seen the last of 'em for tonight," Jeremiah stated. "However, if they show up again I reckon I can handle 'em." He changed the subject. "I been cogitatin' on somethin' son. Seems you and Opal have kind of complicated things by pickin' a day for your wedding that's already a little crowded with celebrations. However, 'pears I have to wish you a Happy New Year, congratulate you on your wedding and wish you a happy birthday all in one mouthful."

"I'm obliged, Pa," Frank said as he headed for the door. He paused there and added, "And Pa, I'm also obliged for the hundred dollars I found on my dresser this morning."

"I wish it could've been more."

Frank returned his father's smile. "I'm going by the Nugget for a bit; I want to make sure Jed's at the wedding tomorrow."

"See you in the morning," Jeremiah answered.

Jeremiah started his final round for the night. He opened the door to the potbellied stove, poked up the embers and tossed in a couple of pieces of wood. As he stood watching for the flame to catch, his mind went back to a New Year's Day twenty-one years ago. "Mattie, how I've missed you! How I wish you were here to see our son married." He sighed aloud. He didn't know whether he thought the words or spoke them aloud, but the pain in his heart was particularly sharp tonight. The wood burst into flame and with a deep sigh he closed the stove, took his sheep-lined coat from a peg, and walked out into the night.

The streets were deserted and the only light shone through the windows of the Nugget Saloon. Because of the inky darkness Jeremiah walked in the center of the street. As he reached the stream of light from the Nugget he glanced through the window and saw Frank talking to Jed, the bartender.

"Marshal!" someone called. Jeremiah stopped when he recognized the voice of Jesse Kreel. "We've got a little unfinished business with you, Marshal."

Jeremiah was framed in the light from the saloon as he began to unbutton his heavy coat.

"Easy Marshal. You just stand there nice and quiet. We'll do the talkin'."

Jeremiah hurled his words into the blackness with all the authority of his office. "Jesse, I told you if you didn't leave town I'd throw you in jail. You're under arrest," he replied as he reached for his gun.

"Hold it, Marshal. Jim is standing about thirty feet from you holdin' a shotgun. You make any foolish moves and he'll blow you in half." Jeremiah heard the smooth click of the shotgun being cocked. "I'd stand mighty still if I were you, Marshal. Jim's a mite drunk and right smart mad about that knot on his head. We don't rightly reckon you had any cause to pistol-whip him thataway. Yessir, bein' I was you I wouldn't move one finger, Jim bein' worked up the way he is and that greener he's holdin' havin' a hair trigger."

At that moment Frank walked out of the saloon

and, seeing his father, he stopped at the edge of the walk. "What's the trouble, Pa?"

Jesse's voice rang out. "Drop your gun, boy! One Applegate at a time is enough!"

Frank could not grasp what was going on. "What is it, Pa?" he asked again.

A gun barked in the darkness and the boardwalk splintered between Frank's feet. "Now, once more, drop your gun," Jesse ordered.

Slowly, Frank lifted his sixshooter and dropped it at his side. At the sound of the gunshot, Jed came running out of the saloon.

"Get down, son!" Jeremiah shouted. He had decided to make his move. With surprising speed, he dropped to the street on his stomach, drawing his gun as he went down. He rolled out of the light and looked for a target. At the same instant, Jed reached for the gun Frank had dropped. The shotgun roared and Jed's hand disappeared. Jeremiah fired at the flash and Jim died with a bullet in his chest. But there was too much to handle. Jesse was running forward, firing as he came, and Jeremiah lost his life because Frank, frozen with fear, could not pick up the gun at his feet and kill the wildly firing Jesse.

Frank's life was spared when Jesse pointed his gun at him and pulled the trigger, the hammer falling on an empty shell. With obvious contempt for the young man, Jesse turned his back and walked to his horse, mounted and rode off.

Jeremiah's funeral was the largest in the memory of the inhabitants of Carson City. Reverend Hetherington conducted the services and praised at great length the man who had been their marshal for so many years. He expressed the sorrow that had struck so close to his family, explaining that his daughter was this day to have married Jeremiah's son. He lamented the senselessness of the murder and urged swift apprehension and punishment of the outlaw who had committed the deed. The small white church on the side of the hill was filled to overflowing with the townspeople, all standing while the preacher offered a prayer for the soul of Jeremiah Applegate. While the small choir sang Nearer the Cross, the coffin was carried through a side door to the cemetery behind the church.

A storm had been building in the northeast and already a few snowflakes were riding the wind and the temperature was dropping. By the time the coffin was lowered to its resting place and the preacher had finished the services, the air was white with snow and wind lashed at the mourners. As they turned to leave, a few of the oldtimers looked apprehensively at the sky and knew they were in for a real bad one.

Frank drew heavily on Opal's strength and he now walked slowly ,by her side toward the parsonage below the church. The storm raged throughout the day and night and snow piled up on the grave of Jeremiah Applegate.

CHAPTER SEVEN
West Against the Wind

Henry's plan was to keep the sun at his back in the morning and follow it across the sky in the afternoon. When the sun rested at night, he rested. He was in no hurry and as the days and miles went by he began to sense the true meaning of his freedom. He was as free as the jays that squawked at him from distant treetops, as free as the trout that swam in the streams where he fished for his breakfast. When the sun was high he would stretch out under a large tree for a daydreaming time.

As he stared up at the great white clouds he would fashion faces and figures of them; a buffalo head or the face of an Indian, a great white stallion or a covered wagon. Just before he dropped off to sleep he would imagine the adventures that lay ahead of him, like meeting some of the great men of the West--Kit Carson, Bill Hickok, Jim Bridger. He dreamed of being an Indian fighter, a prospector, a U.S. cavalryman, or whatever pleased his boyish fancy at the moment.

He stayed clear of towns and people as much as possible except when he ran low on supplies, when he would trade a couple of turkeys or rabbits to a farmer's wife or a storekeeper for what he needed.

As the weeks went by Henry noticed that the terrain had changed. The grass and timberlands had disappeared and the land was flat as far as the eye could see, covered with parched grass and laced with zigzag cracks in the brown earth. Henry's walk west began to lose its excitement as he trudged across the prairie day after endless day. There were no trees for shade and no streams for fishing or bathing. His supplies ran out and the rabbits he shot were as tough as shoe leather. He kept count of the days by tying a knot in a string he extracted from the canvas roll at the end of each day. When they totaled forty, he calculated it must be near the middle of August.
As he was settling down on the pile of tall grass he had pulled up for a bed, he heard dogs barking in the distance. He made note of the direction because it indicated the

presence of a farmhouse and he would seek it out the next morning.

He was up at sunrise, without breakfast, thinking he could work for the farmer for a meal. As the sun rose higher and the landscape came more clearly into view, he stopped in amazement. Only a short distance away was the broadest river he had ever seen. It was wide and muddy and rolling full from bank to bank. And almost on the bank was the farmhouse he had hoped for. He started walking at a brisk pace, hunger gnawing at his insides.

"Hello!" he called from the yard gate.
This was greeted by the barking of a large, liver-spotted dog that charged the gate. Henry backed off and was relieved to see a man coming toward him. He was dressed in the overalls and work shirt of a farmer and Henry greeted him with an anxious, "G'morning. Is that dog a biter or just a barker?" Not very kindly words, Henry decided, so he added, "What river's that there yonder?" Still feeling that he did not have things under control, he followed with, "Would your missus have a likin' for a turkey or a rabbit?" Then, remembering that he had not shot any game for days he added, "Is this here Indiana?" He ended his flow of questions by saying meekly,"My name is Henry Powell and I'm hungry."

The farmer laughed heartily. "Well, Henry Powell, 'pears like you've got a full curiosity and an empty stomach. Reckon maybe we can take care of both. This dog's both a barker and a biter, that's the Mississippi river, we don't need a turkey or a rabbit, and you're in Illinois. Now, if you'll let old Spot here sniff you a few times, chances be right good he'll let you in the kitchen."

Henry got by Spot and stopped at the pump to wash up. Gonna be a good day, he thought. People to talk to and some good home cookin'. When they reached the kitchen the farmer introduced himself.

"I'm Lyman Weatherbee," he said, nodding toward the woman by the stove, "and this is my wife Cynthia. Cynthia, meet Henry Powell."
"Hello, Henry," the woman said as she walked toward the table with a platter of ham. "Pleased to have you sit with us. Don't see many travelers."

Henry suddenly remembered that he had practically come begging. Turning to the man he burst out, "Mr Weatherbee, I'm gonna work for you...I mean, I'm gonna work for this meal if you let me...what I mean is, I can't eat your food less'n I pay you for it or work for it. Got nothin' to pay you with, so I'm hopin' to work for it."

Mr. Weatherbee smiled again. "You're sure a talker once you get started. Wonder if you eat like you talk? Why don't you sit down and let's see. We'll talk about work later."

Remembering his manners, Henry waited until the lady of the house was seated, then he pulled up a chair and looked across the heaping dishes that filled the table. There was a platter of fried eggs, another of skillet-seared ham, a mound of golden butter, a cut-glass dish of strawberry preserves, and right in front of him was a plate piled with hot, oven-browned biscuits. Henry's mouth watered at the delicious smells that rose from the table.
Mrs. Weatherbee folded her hands, lowered her head and started grace. "Dear God, we thank You for that which we are about to partake, and for the guest You have brought to share with us. We pray that...."

The emptiness left Henry's stomach and settled in his chest. How many times he had seen his mother perform the same ritual before a table such as this! He was lost in memories and did not realize Mrs. Weatherbee had finished until Mr. Weatherbee handed him the platter of ham.

"Henry," he said, "for a man who's hungry you're mighty slow to reach."

"I'm sorry," Henry said, "I was thinkin' about somethin'."

"Home?" Mr. Weatherbee questioned. Henry nodded. "Tell us about it." And between mouthfuls of the most wonderful food he'd had in weeks, he did.
Later, Henry helped with some fence-mending, then he cleaned the stables, hoed the garden and did chores around the house. At noon he ate another filling meal. Mr. Weatherbee had convinced him to spend the night and that evening after supper they sat on the side porch in the

evening breeze. "How old are you, Henry?" Mr. Weatherbee asked after he had filled and lighted his pipe.

"Sixteen."

"Look a mite older," the man said.

"I allow a man is as a man does," said Henry.

Mr. Weatherbee continued rocking. "What's this man 'lowin' to do?"

"Goin' west, California maybe," Henry answered.

"Figure it's pretty exciting, do you? Fightin' Indians, diggin' up gold and herdin' cattle?"

"I shore do."

"I felt like you do, once," the man mused aloud. "I got as far as the old Mississip' and stopped at a farm a little north of here, intendin' to work a spell, just like you did, 'ceptin' I married the farmer's daughter and here I be. Wouldn't change it, though, life's been good. I'll leave the ring-tailin' and sky-bustin' to you young colts."

There was a period of silence, the man and the boy each lost in his own thoughts, the peace of the night making it easy to indulge in a little reverie. Finally, Herny rose. "I'm obliged to you and Miz Weatherbee, but I'll be leavin' come mornin'," he said, "that is, can I find a way across that river."

"There's a way," said Mr. Weatherbee, "and when you get across you'll take your first step in what most people consider the West."

"Can't be none too soon," said the boy. "I've come a long way."

Henry went to sleep that night surrounded by the smell of honeysuckle and clover.

The next day, when Mr. Weatherbee hauled Henry across the Mississippi River in his scow, he gave the boy a generous amount of supplies and wished him well.

"Remember, Mrs. Weatherbee has a brother in Jefferson City, Missouri. Bein's you're of mind to, stop by their place for a spell. Jefferson City is three days afoot nigh onto straight west."

Henry's long strides ate up the miles. No longer did he nap in the sun or daydream the hours away. He bedded down at dark, weary from the long day of hiking and slept a restful sleep. He was up at the dawn and had breakfast from his store of supplies, eating while he walked, a solitary figure moving across the vast grasslands of the Missouri prairie. Late in the afternoon of the third day he saw a group of buildings in the distance. He reckoned it to be Jefferson City and asked a man on horseback whom he met at the edge of town.

"It shore is," the rider answered.

Henry proceeded up the main street, looking with keen interest at the many stores on both sides of the dusty street. Dale Forrester was the man he was looking for and he decided the most likely place to get information about the man's whereabouts was at the sheriff's office. He saw a sign marked Sheriff and headed for it.

His hand was on the latch when he happened to see a bulletin board beside the door. Among the number of "Wanted posters tacked on the board was one that read:

WANTED FOR MURDER
HENRY POWELL

Henry froze in his tracks. Below his name was his description. He reread the poster very carefully; the words "Wanted for Murder" slammed into his brain. He couldn't understand it. Sure, he had killed a man, but how could they call it murder? He hadn't done anything wrong; they just didn't understand. Then, from some recess of his mind fear began to creep in. He'd never hand any truck with the law and he had no understanding of such things.

A line in smaller print at the bottom of the poster read, "If this man is apprehended, notify the Logan County Sheriff in Walnut Bend, Ohio at once."

Henry decided to make tracks. He turned and retraced his steps along the road that led him out of town and when he was clear of the buildings he set out across country.

After walking what he considered to be five or six miles, he came upon a grove of cottonwood trees and decided to spend the night there. He had some thinking to do about the awful thing that had happened. He was sure that if he wrote another letter to the sheriff at Walnut

Bend he could explain what had happened and everything would be all right. He decided it was what he would do some day, and with that comforting thought he found a soft spot and fell asleep.

He woke to the smell of coffee cooking. The morning sun was blinding and he could see the silhouette of a man between him and the sunrise.

"G'mornin', young fella. How's for some coffee?"

Henry got up and walked toward the voice. After a closer look he recognized the rider he had met the previous day. "Who might you be?" he asked.

"Harp, I'm known as," said the man as he extended a tin cup.

Henry accepted the brew and squatted down by the fire. "Right kindly of you, but I sure didn't hear you ride in."

"Been here all night," said Harp. "You were sleepin' like a Kentucky coon dog. You gonna wander out here on the plains, you got to learn about self-pertection. If I'd been a 'Sage brave on a hair-liftin' sashay, you'd made easy pickin's."

Henry had nothing to say, so he just stared at Harp through the steam rising from his coffee. He was taken with the man's attire. Harp wore a yellow shirt under a black leather vest adorned town the front with two rows of silver conchos. His black, wide-brimmed hat had a flat crown held down by rawhide thongs knotted under his chin. He wore dark, striped pants and western boots, and snuggled against each hip was an open-ended holster containing a walnut-handled revolver. His face was tanned under a three-day growth of black whiskers and his eyes were black and creased at the corners.

As Henry watched, Harp rolled a cigarette in brown paper, then put it in the corner of his mouth and lit it with a burning twig from the fire. Henry watched, fascinated, A man of the West, he thought. The first honest-to-goodness westerner he had met.

Harp settled back on the ground and crossed his legs under him. "Didn't stay long in town, I notice."

"No reason to," Henry answered. "I'm headin' for California. Which direction might you be goin'?"

"Well now, I travel around a considerable amount. I was headin' into Arkansas country on a job when I passed you yesterday."

Then what are you doing here? Henry thought. Aloud, he said, "What kind of job might that be?"

Harp reached into his shirt pocket and took out a piece of paper, tossing it to Henry. Henry unfolded it and again read the words:

WANTED FOR MURDER
HENRY POWELL

A knot began to grow in the pit of his stomach and he looked questioningly at the man across from him.

"I'm a bounty hunter, kid." Harp tossed his cigarette into the fire and stood up. "Local sheriff tells me Henry Powell's worth a hundred dollars. Tain't much, but I reckon I can take a few hours to drop a loop on a greenhorn kid for an easy hundred dollars. That description pretty well pegs you as Henry Powell. Am I right, kid?"

Henry stood up and dropped the paper into the fire. "Yes, I'm Henry Powell," he answered.

"Get your things together; we're heading for Jefferson City." Unable to think of anything else to do, Henry complied. "You can swing up in front of me," said Harp, "or go it afoot. Suit yourself."

"I'll walk," said Henry.

"Then start walkin'," Harp ordered.

Henry started back the way he had come the day before, with Harp riding twenty or thirty feet behind. Harp had Henry's old rifle lying across the saddle in front of him and he began to inspect it with the natural curiosity of a man who makes his living with a gun. After a few minutes Henry stopped and waited for Harp to catch up.

"What do you reckon will come of all this?" he asked his captor.

Harp swung the long-barrelled gun to his shoulder and sighted off into the distance at an imaginary target. "Mighty formidable weapon you carry, boy." With his cheek still nestled against the stock, he continued, "This what you used to kill that man?"

"No," Henry replied.

Lowering the gun, Harp said, "Then you did murder him."

"I killed him but it warn't murder."

"So be it, my young friend, but I still 'low as they'll hang you. Now, let's get movin'."

Henry started off again, filled with confusion and frustration. They had gone about a quarter of a mile when he stopped again and turned to face Harp. "I ain't goin' no further," he said.

Harp lifted his gun from its holster and leveled it at Henry. "Look, kid," he said, "I don't want to have to take you in town with a hole in you, but I got no time to fool around. Now let's get goin'."

"I ain't goin no further," Henry repeated.

Harp was taken aback. He had no stomach to shoot down a boy over a measly hundred dollars. Holstering his gun, he reached for his lariat, another plan in mind.

Henry decided it was time to make his move. He slid under the horse, wrapping his arms around it's front legs and gave a mighty heave with his massive shoulders. Horse and rider crashed to the ground, but the animal quickly scrambled to its feet, leaving Harp stunned and lying in the grass. Henry lifted the guns from Harp's holsters and was relieved to note that the man was still breathing.

When Harp finally came around he tried to rise and grimaced in pain. "My leg's busted," he groaned. "Lordy-God, you're a ringtailed wildcat when you cut loose! I'd a been smart to've kept headin' for Arkansas. Now I'll be laid up a month. You plannin' to help me or shoot me? Way this leg is a-painin', wish you'd do one or the other."

Henry retrieved his rifle and took Harp's lariat, then set to work to do what he could for the injured man. First, he grasped Harp's ankle and with a quick jerk snapped the broken bone into place; Harp howled with pain and cursed. Then, using the rifle barrel as a splint, he bound it to Harp's leg with the rope. With little effort, he picked the man up and headed for the cottonwood grove.

Minutes later, as they rested in the shade, Henry studied the situation. "I plumb don't know what to do with you," he finally said.
Harp's breathing was labored and he was obviously in pain. "You sure got yourself a problem, boy. 'Lowin' you don't come up with an answer, might be I'll have a suggestion to make."

Henry got to his feet and stood staring off to the west. Harp knew the thoughts he must be playing with.
"You leave me here, boy, and I'll die, and you'll have killed another man. Now, you don't want to do that."

Henry stood silent for a long time. Finally he turned and squatted down by the prone figure. "I declare, Harp, I can't untangle this ball o' twine. Guess I'm ready to listen to your idea."

Harp looked into the face of the young man before him. He saw wide-set blue eyes tormented with worry and the corners of the sensitive mouth were drawn down with concern over the man-sized problem facing him. Harp could not associate "murderer" with the youngster before him. "Let's start this way, but first, I want to show you something." He pulled up his right sleeve to show Henry a Derringer strapped to his forearm. "I could have shot you a dozen times over the last half hour, the point bein' when you down a man search him for hide-out weapons; you'll live a spell longer if you do.

"Fact is, you're so green, boy, I don't calculate you'll ever make California. You're headin' into Indian country and you gotta cross the Cherokee Nation. Further on there's Comanches, Sioux and "Paches. Why, boy, if you don't know how to handle yourself they'll pounce on you like a coyote on a quail. There's towns like Dodge City, Wichita and Santa Fe filled with gunslingers who would as leave shoot you as ask your name. However, that's another problem.

"My plan ought to work out right well for both of us. You round up my hoss and bring it here. There's a quart of liquor in the saddlebag that'll knock the edge off the pain in my busted leg. Then you ride into town and leave word at Doc Simmons' office that I'm out here. If you can see to do that, I'll make a deal with you. In return for the favor and this ol' rifle strapped to my leg, I'll give you my hoss and saddle. That way you got half a chance of gettin' across Indian country. There just ain't no other way for both of us to pull outta this. 'Course, you could just ride off on your own, but then you'd be a hoss thief and out here, stealin' a hoss is worse'n killin' a man. How's it sound? We got a deal?"

"Reckon so," Henry agreed. " I can't think of anythin' better."

A few days later, Henry rode into Wichita on Harp's big Appaloosa. He entered the town from the east and looked down the longest street he had ever seen. It was teeming with people, on horseback and in wagons of all shapes and sizes, or treading the boardwalks that lined both sides of the street. Forgotten was his hunger and his fear of the Wanted poster. He rode slowly along the dirt street, taking in all the sights his eyes could gather. He stopped to watch a medicine man working from the tailgate of a small covered wagon.

"Why, folks," the man was saying, "there just ain't no disease or ailment attackin' man or beast that Dr. Markham's Magic Remedy can't handle. It'll cure bunions and baldness, the hives and the heaves, backache, bellyache and boils." On and on, the huckster mesmerized his audience and was soon doing a thriving business at a dollar the bottle.

On down the street, Henry watched an auction taking place. Along the edge of the street were two teams of broad-backed gray horses hitched to a conestoga wagon. The canvas was rolled up on the sides, exposing a load of household goods. Beside the wagon was an assortment of farm implements. The auctioneer was standing on a barrel in front of the lead team. To the side, in a straight-backed chair, a small woman sat, her face hidden by the brim of her sunbonnet.

"Ladies and gentlemen, we're gonna auction off here today four of the finest horses ever to put a hoof west of the Mississippi, and with them, a wagon hand-crafted from seasoned oak and hickory, a wagon that will last any man's lifetime. There's tools and furnishin's and household items of the finest quality. We're gonna sell it all here today. The terms are cash and all sales are final."

The man lowered his voice. "This dear lady sitting before you has lost her beloved husband. Russell Severson was a good man and some of you knew him. He brought his wife across a thousand miles, intendin' to homestead further west, but outside Wichita he took sick. What with, only the good Lord knows, but it killed him and now all his widow has on this earth are these belongin's you see before you. This poor woman needs all the money she can get, so I don't want no mollycoddling shenanigans in the bidding. Speak up and cut the corners square."

Henry nudged the Appaloosa and moved to the rear of the wagon where he dismounted and tied the reins to the high rear wheel. He started working his way between the edge of the crowd and the side of the wagon, but he was blocked after he had moved a short distance. Then he noticed the "lazy board" had been pulled out a foot or two from the side of the wagon. Pulling himself up onto it, he squatted down to get a good view over the heads of the crowd.

The auctioneer was warming to his work. "You gents step up an look over these horses. They're sound as a dollar. They run sixteen and a half hands and just a mite under two thousand pounds apiece. They're matched five-year olds and just to make you a good deal, the harness goes with 'em. Now, gentlemen, who'll give me a bid for these four beauties?"

Somewhere in the crowd a man called out, "five hundred!"

The auctioneer started his chant and Henry thought it was prettier than any song he'd ever heard. "Five hundred, I'm bid, who'll make it six? Five, five, I'm bid, who'll go six? Six, six I need, who'll bid six? Five I've got, looking for six."

From the far side of the crowd a hand went up and the bid went to six hundred. The auctioneer continued, calling now for a bid of seven hundred. Someone close to Henry called out, "Seven hundred!"
The auctioneer's chant gained momentum. Words rolled from his mouth like glass marbles of sound. Faster and

faster came the call. The buyers got caught up in the fever of bidding and the figure rose to eight hundred, eight-fifty, then nine-fifty. The auctioneer sensed he had nearly reached the top and with a disturbing suddenness he cut off his stream of words in mid-sentence. Henry felt suddenly uncomfortable.

The auctioneer took a blue bandana out of his coat pocket and wiped his face, then motioned to his assistant, who handed him a dipper of water. He studied the crowd as he drank. Then, after putting his handkerchief back in his coat pocket, he pulled a big gold watch from his vest pocket. "I want to hear a thousand dollar bid in the next sixty seconds, else we're gonna sell these horses separately." He stood staring at his watch.

Henry was enjoying the excitement. He stared at each of the bidders. Would one of them pay the thousand dollars, he wondered? All cash, the man had said. Wouldn't it be something to see a thousand dollars in cash?

"I'll bid a thousand," a man called out. The auctioneer pocketed his watch and pointed toward the man. "Sold to that gentleman for one thousand dollars! What's your name, sir?"

"The United States Army," was the answer.

"All right, Mister United States Army, you've bought yourself some top horseflesh. Now, sir, would you like to make the first bid on the wagon?"

"I'll bid one thousand dollars."

"That's a fine start," said the auctioneer. Again he began to work the crowd with his rapid-fire plea for a higher price, but not a single bid was forthcoming. "Sold to the man for one thousand dollars," he said.

Henry took a closer look at the buyer as he talked with a small man at his side. He was a large, untidy individual and his face was covered with two or three day's growth of beard. His shirt sleeves were rolled to the elbow, exposing massive forearms burned brown by the sun, each with a number of scars lighter in color and completely devoid of the long, black hair that covered the rest of his arms. He wore dark, ill fitting pants held up by Army-issue galluses. A coiled bullwhip hung from a wire hook looped onto his trouser top. It was braided leather with a hickory handle and from the end hung a long rawhide popper.

"Your team and rig will be ready in an hour," the auctioneer called.

"I'm takin' 'em now," the buyer said. "Get that wagon unloaded."

"I had planned to sell the contents from the floor of the wagon," the auctioneer objected.

"You just had a change of plans. Get that junk outta there or it goes with me!"

The woman in the chair gazed up at the man in amazement. She spoke a few low words to the auctioneer and he soon had a group of men unloading her belongings under a tree. In the meantime, the new owner paid his money and received a receipt made out to "J.T. Harris, Supplier to the United States Army". His companion, a wiry little individual, was looking over the horses. It was plain to see that he knew horses by the gentle way he ran his fingers over their withers and forelegs. He answered to the name of "Scat" when the larger man ordered him into the wagon.

J.T. Harris was "Mule" Harris to the rest of the world, but to Scat he was always "Mister Harris". In the same breath that Scat was ordered into the wagon, words were bellowed at Henry. "Hit the dirt boy. You're on my property!" Henry dropped to the ground, untied his horse and mounted.

He was never sure what spooked the Appaloosa, but something did, for suddenly things started to happen. His horse leaped into a dead run in the direction he happened to be headed, which was straight at the broad back of Mule Harris. Henry tried desperately to rein away, but it was too late and they crashed into the big man. Mule was slammed against the wheel of the wagon and fell to his knees. The Appaloosa reared up and when he came down, his left foreleg became entangled in the team harness. The big horses laid their ears back and shied away, while the Appaloosa pranced and bucked and Henry hung on for dear life.

The front team finally wound up on the boardwalk, some of the men there grabbing their bits and finally calmed them down. But Henry's Appaloosa could not free himself and was thrashing in panic. Regaining his seat Henry began to talk to his mount and stroke his arched neck.

Just then, there was a crack like a rifle shot and a long red slash appeared on the horse's neck. Henry watched in astonishment as the blood began to run. A second crack and another cut appeared close to the first one. The horse trembled in fear and pain and Henry looked to his left in time to see Mule Harris send the bullwhip singing through the air a third time. The rawhide cracked and Henry's leg was laid open just above the knee.

Henry left the saddle in an awkward lunge and landed on all fours as the bullwhip cracked above him. He rushed his assailant as Mule raised his arm for another stroke, twisted the whip loose and threw it into the crowd.

Mule jerked his arm free and stepped back to appraise the new development. Henry did not know what to expect so he stood and waited. Some of the men had untangled his horse and were giving their attention to the wounds on its neck. The big horses had settled down and order was being restored.

Henry could feel the blood from the cut on his leg running into his boot and anger pounded in his chest. "You didn't have any call to do that, Mister!" he said.

"Sonny," Mule answered, "best you leave your name with someone to take to your ma, 'cause when I get through with you, you're gonna be under six feet o' dirt." With that he put his hat on the rim of the wagon wheel and started toward Henry.

The story of the hand-to-hand battle that took place between the two men in the dusty street of Wichita, Kansas on that hot August afternoon was told to children and grandchildren for years afterward. They were men of great strength, angry and fighting for their pride.

They fought with fists and feet, they butted and kneed and gouged and clawed. One of Mule's favorite ways of fighting was to clasp his hands in front of him and with his elbows out, swing them back and forth like a giant scythe. His elbows were like gnarled oak and when one of them crashed into the side of Henry's head, Henry thought the world had exploded. He fell against Mule, wrapped his arms around his waist in a bear hug and squeezed as hard as he could. He could feel the powerful muscles in Mule's back straining to fend off the tremendous pressure. With a man of lesser strength, the grip would have broken his back.

Mule spread his feet and, twisting his body once again, sent his elbow flush against Henry's ear like a battering ram. Henry dropped to the street. Before his senses cleared, he instinctively reached out to grab Mule's leg and jerked it forward. The big man toppled and Henry raised his knee just in time to catch his opponent full in the face. Mule's features splattered with the sound of a rock being dropped into thick mud. Both men were a trifle slower this time in getting to their feet; Mule had blood streaming from his nose and his mouth and Henry's head rang with a hundred bells.

They lunged at each other again and again, on into the afternoon, from one side of the street to the other. Their clothes were torn and covered with blood as they punished each other in any manner that entered their heads. For a while it seemed their strength was equally matched and the fight would not end until both men were dead, but as shadows crept across the street, it became apparent that Mule was rising a little more slowly and seemed less eager to continue than he had at the start.

Suddenly, Henry's anger was sated and he wanted the fight ended, which made him careless.

Mule kicked hard at the cut on Henry's leg and when Henry doubled over in pain, Mule brought both massive fists down with crushing force on the back of his head. Henry dropped to the ground and rolled over on his back and Mule fell on him, wrapping his hands around Henry's throat, his long thumbs cutting deeply into Henry's flesh. Henry knew if he backed out he would never see daylight again, so he grabbed Mule's head, placing one hand on the man's chin and the other on the back of his neck and twisting hard and fast. He felt the click of bones snapping and the pressure on his throat was relieved instantly. Mule's body sank against him like a large sack of grain.

Henry shoved the dead weight off and got to his feet. He looked down at the man whose neck he had just broken and was sorry he did. Mule was lying flat on his stomach and Henry was looking full into the dead man's face. It dawned on him then that he had just killed another man.

He washed at a watering trough as best he could. The shirt he had worn all the way from Ohio, homemade muslin and stained with walnut juice, hung in tatters. His pants were covered with dirt and caked with blood. The only things worth keeping were his belt and boots. The belt was fashioned of thin strips of muskrat hide and the boots he had had made in Walnut Bend with uppers of black and white calf hide from an animal butchered on the farm.

Henry was busy scrubbing when he became aware of someone standing behind him. He turned to look down at a very small man wearing two very large guns on his hips and a star on his vest. He was backed by three thin, hawk-faced, disreputable-looking individuals.

The undersized sheriff looked Henry over from head to toe. An image of the Wanted poster surges through Henry's mind, but the sheriff's words put to rest any fears on that score. "Welcome to Wichita, big man," he said, "or should I say, big boy? How old are you?"

"Twenty," Henry lied.

"Could be," the sheriff agreed. "Quite a scrap you put up. The man you killed wasn't the best-liked man in Wichita, by a damn sight."

"I'm real sorry it happened," Henry returned.

"Don't be," said the sheriff. "Mule Harris thought he was boss dog with that bullwhip. Many a man that's been bit with that blacksnake has hankered to put a bullet in Mule's carcass. You're gonna be a real hero around here, so don't you go feelin' bad about it a-tall. By the way, what's your handle, anyway?"

"Henry," he began, then remembering the poster he added, "Logan."

"All right, Henry Logan, you come on over to the office

and we'll make up a legal report concerning the sudden demise of Mister Harris. I'm Thurgood Curtis, sheriff of Wichita, known by most hereabouts as "Goody". And seein' as how you were attacked with a lethal weapon, namely a bullwhip, I reckon the judge is goin' to see it as self defense."

Following the sheriff, his ragged shirt clutched in one hand, Henry went through the crowd to the sheriff's office. He heard kindly comments from various people on the way and one man stopped him to say that his horse had been taken to Judson's Livery Stable on Second Street. Henry paused to thank him and when he turned back to follow the sheriff, he came face to face with the mousy little man Mule had called Scat.

"I hanker to talk to you, Mister," said Scat, "'lowin' the sheriff don't lock you up, which I mighty sure hope he don't. Fact is, I got a proposition that I reckon ought to listen pretty good to a young feller like you." Scat interrupted his rapid-fire chewing for a moment to offer Henry a brown smile of tobacco-stained teeth.

There was too much on Henry's mind to work up an answer so he pushed by the little man. However, when he went in the sheriff's office he noticed Scat in a chair outside the door.

An hour later, Henry and Scat were seated at a table in a corner of the Cattlemen's Saloon two blocks west of the sheriff's office. The sheriff had given Henry a shirt left by a prisoner who had played the star role in a hanging. It was too small, but it would do until he could make other arrangements.

The "other arrangements" were well under way because Scat wanted to take Henry on as a partner. "We can make us a heap of money, Mister Logan, but we've got to head for Fort Dodge come sunup. Why, we can haul five tons of supplies with that rig Mister Harris bought. The stuff's all stacked and waitin' at the stage depot. There's a hundred cases of Winchesters, fifty of Spencers, fifty kegs of gunpowder, two hundred bars of lead, and a tolerable 'glomeration of other supplies. In a holdin' corral at the edge of town, there's eleven mules, twenty milk cows and a half dozen Indian ponies. The general at Fort

Dodge is a-troublin' himself right smart to get these supplies in. Mister Harris and I been supplyin' the forts hereabouts for two-three years now and we done right well by ourselves, too. With Mister Harris about to be laid away, howsoever, I need a partner and I'm puttin' that offer to you, be you willin'."

Henry had heard enough to know it was a way to get further west and a chance to make some money. "Well," he said, "I'm needin' my leg patched up and some new duds and two or three plates of beans. Might be your deal'd sound fine then."

"Said is done," Scat answered. "After the ruckus in the street I lifted Mister Harris' poke. Half'n it was mine anyway. We'll get your needs cared for pronto."

Scat called for a bottle and poured Henry his very first drink of rye whiskey. He liked the burn of the fiery liquid as it slid down his throat and landed in his empty stomach with a small explosion. He felt runners of warmth shoot through his body and finally settle in a big smile on his face. He felt good and relaxed, with a sense of well-being. If such pleasant feelings and immediate happiness were corked up in a bottle called "rye whiskey", he'd have to have another drink some day, he decided.

Scat hired a couple of worn-out cowboys to help him herd the cattle, and when the sun polished the tall grass the next morning, they were on their way. Henry was dressed in the traditional striped gambler's pants with a buckskin shirt and a Stetson hat. He carried a Spencer repeating rifle across his saddle and he and his Appaloosa led out a hundred yards ahead of the wagon. Scat handled the reins of the team, walking beside the front wheel since there was no seat on the Conestoga. The only sounds to be heard were the squeak of the harness under strain and the creaks and groans of the rumbling wagon. Henry looked back over his shoulder and felt that at last he had become a part of the West.

CHAPTER EIGHT
The Making of a Killer

The sun rose the following morning with an abruptness possible only in northern New Mexico. Tom joined Crimp for his breakfast beans, so named by Crimp because he tossed two fried eggs into a plate of beans. Crimp's coffee was so black that a few swallows brought a man awake in a hurry.

"Today you're gonna learn to shoot," Crimp announced. "As soon as you've finished the chores, meet me out back."

Later, when Tom walked out to the corral, Crimp was nailing a horseshoe to the wood fence about five feet off the ground. "All I want you to do is put every shot inside that horseshoe. It's about shirt pocket high and the right size. I'm not as good as I once was, but I'll try to show you what I have in mind."
Tom could hardly tell which came first, the blur of movement or the blast of the three shots. Almost in the center of the horseshoe were three holes. "Holy Moly!" he exclaimed.

"You'll be doing that, boy, when ol' Crimp gets finished with you. Now go move the shoe and we'll see what you can do."

Tom's first draw missed by a yard. He drew and fired until his arm ached and the wood fence was peppered with holes, but the surface inside the horseshoe remained untouched. Crimp gave a word of advice now and then and an hour later, the holes began to move closer to the shoe. Tom had learned the trick of bunching his muscles a split second before he grabbed for his gun and he could palm and trigger the gun before he realized it had happened. Now, he decided to allow his mind to become detached from his will and on the next draw, to his amazement and without any apparent effort on his part, a hole appeared dead center in the horseshoe.

"Put it up," said Crimp. "That'll do for today."

"How did that last one suit you?" Tom asked with a smile of pride.

Crimp neither answered nor smiled. Instead, he stared at Tom for a long moment, realizing that he had created a deadly, determined killer. Crimp remembered his own compulsion to try out every gunman he met. It was a sickness and already Tom was showing the first symptoms.

"Go get drunk or go fishin' or do some damn thing; just get the hell out of my sight for awhile," he said as he disappeared into the stable.

Tom turned back to the horseshoe. He drew and another hole appeared close to the first. A feeling of power swept over him. He slid his gun back into the holster and took the cartridge with Will Storm's name on it from his shirt pocket. He tossed the round into the air, caught it in his shirt pocket, then headed for Dugan's Saloon. What happened over the next forty-eight hours Crimp never knew because he did not ask and Tom did not say.

Two days later, Tom spent the next session on the firing line alone and Crimp's absence was an admission that he had no more to teach his young pupil. Tom fired less than a dozen rounds with unerring accuracy. Whatever it was that comprised the ultimate skill of a fast-draw gunhand, Tom had acquired it.

At dawn the next morning Tom shook Crimp awake. "Reckon I'll be movin' on," he said. "I'm hankerin' to have me a look at the Arizona Territory. I reckon I ought to..."

"Damnation," Crimp interrupted. "Don't you go thankin' me, boy. What I did for you ain't nothin' a man ought to be thanked for. Teachin' you to be a fast gun warn't no favor to you. Afore you're through you'll despise the day you ever met me."

Tom's left hand shot out at a speck moving in the light from the window. "Naw," he said, "you just made me the world's fastest flycatcher." With a smile he dropped the fly on Crimp's chest. "Likely I'll be back this way one day," he added as he walked out.

"Not a chance," Crimp murmured to himself. "Not a potbellied chance.

Tom rode out of the rolling hills and rock country

into Deming, New Mexico one evening at sundown. He stabled his horse and headed for a saloon to quench a three-day thirst. As his footsteps echoed on the wooden walk in the almost deserted street, an uneasiness crept over him, different from the feeling he had when he visited other towns. It did not dawn on him that he was now a different man.

Evening settled over the town, which had been completely subdued by the hammering heat of the day, and with the coolness came the peculiar quiet that precedes darkness. In the strange silence broken only by the sound of his own footsteps, Tom felt he was the sole occupant of a deserted town. Then, slowly, the sounds of the night began to move in. From one direction he heard a door slam, from another a mother scolded her children, and then, the sound he was searching for, piano music and the ring of feminine laughter. He increased his gait and soon passed through the swinging doors of the Red Star Saloon.

He stopped just inside the swinging doors and surveyed the room. Already he was acquiring the caution of a gunfighter. He was looking for guns worn low, tied-down holsters, gloved hands, or men who seemed to be loners. If there were a possible adversary in the room he wanted to know it now. He was following advice Crimp had pounded into his head repeatedly.

Satisfied with his inspection, he chose a table by the wall and settled into a chair facing the door. He studied the waitress as she approached. She was wearing a faded red dress of soft material that exposed much of her breasts and most of her legs. Her face, probably beautiful once, was now heavy with makeup, attempting to cover a few wrinkles and a multitude of disappointments. Even so, her perfume was a pleasant contrast to the smell of smoke, sweat and beer that hung heavy in the room.

"What'll it be, cowboy?"

Tom ignored the question. "Fella I know...wonder if he's passed through here, name of Will Storms."

"I sell beer and booze, buster. Information you get from Bodie."

"And who might Bodie be?"

"He owns this here palace of pleasure."

"Reckon I could talk to him?" Tom queried.

"Reckon so; he's standing at the end of the bar. You drinkin' or ain't you?"

"At the bar, sweetheart, right next to Mister Bodie."

E.J. Bodie was a heavy man with a fleshy face, watery eyes and an insatiable appetite for long, black cigars. Most of the time he stood at the end of the bar, fingering the gold nugget attached to a chain across his protruding stomach and watching with obvious pleasure the flow of money pouring into the cash register. He wore a black hat square on his head and his bushy mustache bobbed as he shifted his cigar from one corner of his mouth to the other.

Tom took a spot next to the corpulent proprietor. "My pleasure if you'd join me in a drink, Mister Bodie."

The cigar stopped in the off-side corner while the smoker appraised Tom and his invitation. Tom took advantage of it to order a bottle of rye and two glasses. When the bartender saw Tom slide one of the glasses in front of his employer, he reached under the bar for the bottle from which he filled the boss' glass.

Tom smiled understandingly, filled his own glass and raised it as he turned to his guest. "To your health, sir," he said. He paused halfway through his drink to watch with fascination while Bodie downed his drink without removing the cigar.

"You got something to sell, you want a job, or you're lookin' for somebody and Belle said to ask me. Likely I can help you with any one of them," he said as he mopped his face with a handkerchief.

"I'm looking for a man calls himself Will Storms."

At an almost imperceptible nod from Bodie, the bartender filled both his glass and Tom's. The two men drank and from the smooth taste of the liquor, Tom appreciated why the proprietor had his own private stock. Out came the handkerchief again, followed by a question. "This man a friend of yours?"

"First off, he ain't rightly a man, he's a yellow-bellied skunk, and secondly, he's no friend of mine."

"He's a friend of mine."

The words came from behind him and Tom turned

slowly to see who spoke them. The man's clothes were sweat-stained and dust-covered and he had a week's growth of beard. The only thing about him that seemed to have any life at all was his unblinking eyes. "Like I said, cowboy, Will Storms is a friend of mine and I don't rightly like to hear him called a yellow-bellied skunk, especially when he ain't around to hear it, and especially from a big-mouth greenhorn like you."

Tom felt an excitement he had never known before. The man facing him was a gunfighter, he had no doubt about that. The stranger spoke again.

"Let's suppose I'm Will Storms. What did you have in mind doing, big mouth?"

"If you was Will Storms, I'd kill you. But you ain't so I got no call to draw on you Mister, less'n you push it."

"Where in tarnation did you get the idea that you could stand up against Will Storms?"

"Friend of mine name of Crimp 'lowed I could hold my own."

"Crimp Madsen?"

"The same."

A marked change came over the stranger. "People call me R.D. I knew Crimp in the old days and 'lowin' he's a friend of yours, reckon I spoke a mite hasty."

"Apology accepted," Tom replies. "Step up and cut the dust. Mister Bodie serves mighty fine liquor."

"No apology intended," R.D. protested. "Fact is, I was wonderin', did Crimp teach you how to shoot or talk?"

"Well now, I reckon there's only one way to find out, Mister."

R.D. was still uncertain since the name of Crimp Madsen had come up. "Ain't no sense for you and me to be shootin' holes in each other, kid. I got a better idea." Turning to the bartender he said, "I 'low you got a candle back there somewheres. Stick it in the neck of a bottle, light it and set it at the far end of the bar."
At a nod of permission from Bodie, the bartender did as he was asked.

"And now, my young friend, the barkeep's goin' to toss a coin in the air. When it hits the bar, we draw." He laid a twenty-dollar gold piece on the bar and turned to

Bodie. "You cover this gold, winner takes all?" Again a nod and the bartender selected a coin from the cash register.

The coin spun through the air and when it hit the bar, the candle was out and Tom stood with a smoking gun in his hand. R.D. was frozen in position, his forty-four barely half out of the holster. He stared, as did everyone else in the room. Bodie's mouth hung open and his cigar dropped to the floor as he stared at the candle. Tom drew the spent cartridge out of the cylinder with slow deliberation and thumbed in a fresh one.

R.D. put his gun back into the holster and stared at the gun in Tom's hand for a few seconds, then looked into Tom's face. As if talking to himself, he exclaimed, "Great Godalmighty!" Fear, admiration and awe moved him to ask, "Who might I tell Will is lookin' for him?"

"Tom Pender's the name and there's somethin' else you can tell him." From his shirt pocket he took the cartridge and turned it so R.D. could read the inscription. "Tell him I'm savin' this for him." Tom picked up the coins and dropped them in his pocket with the cartridge.

Familiar sounds began to return to the room and some of the men moved back to the bar. "I'd be right pleased to have that drink now," R.D. said.

"Help yourself," Tom invited. "I have a little more business with Mister Bodie." He moved next to the shaken owner of the Red Star. "You mentioned jobs a minute ago, Mister Bodie. Might it be you could direct a feller to a drive or an outfit that's hirin' on? I'm runnin' a little low on scratch."

"Might be," was the answer. Mister Bodie placed the end of his cigar in the chimney of a lamp and puffed hard for a light. "Fact is," he continued, "I'm gettin' five dollars a head for every rider I send to Red Scanlon. He's plannin' a drive out of Mexico. If you're interested, sign on with Red at Tubac, Arizona Territory. He's pullin' out for the border Saturday next. That's six days, but you can ride it in five, allowin' that you leave come morning."

"You just earned five dollars Mister Bodie, and I'm obliged." Tom slopped his glass full, downed it and headed for the door. He gave Belle a pat on the rump as he went by and looked back at R.D., whose eyes followed him all the way. "Adios, amigo," he said.

"Adios, Tom Pender. I hope to be around when you meet up with Will Storms. I'd shore hate to miss that."

Tom washed up in the livery stable watering trough, then crawled into the haymow to enjoy a dreamless sleep.

When he left the next morning, the eastern sky was a sheet of gold and not a soul did he see as he rode down the center of the quiet, dusty street. As he passed the last house, he caught the belly-clenching odor of bacon frying. With only the prospect of fried rabbit for breakfast, Tom had half a notion to drop in, but he heeled the buckskin instead, hoping to cover a number of miles in the cool of the morning. He didn't know it, but he was headed for the town of Buell, Arizona.

CHAPTER NINE
L Troop, D Company

The long trip to Fort Dodge took twenty days. One or two small Indian scouting parties, probably Kiowa, stayed at a distance, watching them pass and then disappearing over the horizon. The journey was so uneventful that Henry acquired an addiction to Scat's chewing tobacco. He filled his mouth with the sweet leaves every morning after breakfast and chewed and spat the two hundred miles to Fort Dodge.

Fort Dodge was built of adobe and Henry could see it in the distance, on the banks of the Arkansas River where the Santa Fe Trail turned south. It was a walled fort with a number of buildings outside the walls. They were the beginning of what some day would be known as Dodge City, Kansas.

Fort Dodge had been built a year or two earlier as a base of operations against the marauding Arapaho and Cheyenne under the command of General Miles. From Fort Dodge, George Armstrong Custer was to head a contingent of United States Cavalry in his obsession to win fame and glory on the western frontier. Henry was to miss by one week witnessing the arrival of the man who would die one day on a bloody knoll at the Little Big Horn.

As they approached the fort, Henry saw several stacks of something he could not identify. "Them's buffler hides," Scat explained. "We'll be haulin' all of 'em we can load back to the railhead at Saint Joe. We can get five dollars gold for every ten hides we freight. 'Low we can haul a couple of thousand, then we'll hightail it back with another load of rifles and powder for the Army. Yessir, Mister Logan, we'll rest over two-three days, then we'll shuck out for Missouri."

But Henry had other plans. He would draw his cut and stay on at Fort Dodge until spring. He told Scat when the soldiers had unloaded that wagon that night.

The winter months passed slowly and Henry's restlessness grew irritating to those around him. It was a relief to everyone when he rode out near the middle of

May. After he left the safety of Fort Dodge, his plan was to sleep by day and ride by night. His plan succeeded because, other than a cavalry scouting party returning to Fort Dodge, he met no one and on the afternoon of the fifth day he rode into Fort Bent.

Fort Bent was built of stone with walls fifteen feet high, on the banks of a river at the base of a small mountain. As Henry rode up to the entrance, he heard band music from over the walls. He was stopped by a sentry and after being granted permission to enter, the gate was opened for him. He could see that some sort of ceremony was underway. "What is it?" he asked a soldier by the gate.

"A military funeral, sir. Keep to the inside wall until you reach the stables."

It was May 24th, 1868, and the funeral was the first ceremony of its kind conducted at the new Fort Bent. The compound was filled with cavalrymen standing at attention in lines that reached from one end of the fort to the other. The bright blue color of their uniforms was broken only by the wide gold stripe on their trousers and the sunlight glinting on brass insignia. Each company had a brightly-colored guidon moving in the gentle breeze.

The regimental band was stationed in the far corner playing a military hymn. In the shade of a piece of canvas held up by four poles was a caisson drawn by four chestnut horses. The front off horse bore a soldier in a full dress uniform who sat holding a sword with the tip pointing upward. On the caisson was a casket draped with the American flag. Abruptly, the music stopped and there was a long period of silence.

Henry reined his horse to a stop and sat watching the pageantry. A short line of officers had been standing facing the caisson. Suddenly, one of them did a brisk about-face, marched eight precise steps and stopped. His orders rang out and reverberated from wall to wall.

"Pre-sent...arms!"
The muffled sound of six hundred rifles being lifted to position was an act of military precision.

"Honor Guard, shoul-der...arms! Right...face! Forward half time...march!"

A squad of sixteen men marching with the hesitation step headed for the gate and the small cemetery outside the walls of the fort. Four drummers, their drums muffled with black cloth, and four buglers fell in behind the caisson. As it moved out, the drummers beat a cadence with rolling monotony.

The officers completed the procession and as it moved past, Henry felt prickles of gooseflesh from head to toe. He did not move until the entire entourage had passed through the gate, then he sat for awhile, musing upon what he had seen. Finally, he rode to the far end of the compound where he had seen a hitching rail. He was about to dismount when a sound came to his ears that held him in the saddle. From outside the walls came the first notes of Taps. As the bugler finished the first bar, a second bugler played the echo, then a third and a fourth. The notes were so sweet, clear and golden that Henry felt a lump come up in his throat. The notes rained into the compound like the tears of God. Gradually, the first bugler finished, then the second, third and fourth, until the final notes drifted away to lose themselves across the river and stillness again engulfed the fort.

Henry tied up to the rail and walked slowly toward the stables. He questioned a corporal at the stable door. "Who did they bury out there today?"

"Kit Carson," the man answered.

The corporal eyed Henry in silence for a long moment, seeing him as a recruit. "The United States Cavalry will take twenty-four hours of your time every day. You'll ride out on forays from two to six weeks at a time, when the sun'll be hotter than the side walls of hell. You'll live on dust and black coffee; you'll sleep on rocky ground with a rattlesnake for a bed partner', you'll be expected to fight Indians as long as there are Indians--and there's one hell of a lot of them; you'll likely take a few bullets in your carcass or an arrow in your brisket; and for this you'll be paid thirteen dollars a month and a ration of tobacco, an issue of clothing and blankets, a horse and a rifle. If this sounds like a pot you'd like to cut, put your John Henry on the bottom line."

Henry was standing at the adjutant's desk outside the General's office. A lot had happened since he had arrived at Fort Bent three weeks ago. He had taken a liking to the Colorado Territory and his thoughts of California had faded considerably. He had met some of the men and decided he liked their carefree way of life.

As he watched L Troop ride through the big gate with flags and guidons snapping in the breeze this morning, he felt a longing to go with them. They were singing "The Girl I left Behind Me", and as the song followed them into the distance, Henry knew he wanted to become a U.S. Cavalryman. "Sir," he said to the adjutant, "I have a couple of request in mind."

"Spit 'em out," was the stern reply.

"Well, sir, I'd be right proud and obliged were I to be assigned to L Troop."

"We'll make note of it," said the adjutant, "but you picked the toughest, fightin'est bunch of Indian-haters in any fort in the West. Any one of 'em would chase an Indian barefooted straight into Hades, stab him to death with the Devil's tail and roast his ears in the fires of Hell. You plan on sharin' biscuits with those boys, you'll damn soon learn that soldierin' is butt-bustin work. What's the other thing in your craw?"

"I want to keep that Appaloosa I rode in on."

The adjutant leaned back in his chair. "Can't be boy. Every man in L Troop rides a bay. You want L Troop, you exchange that Indian pony for a bay. What'll it be?"

"I'll take L Troop," Henry replied without hesitation.

"Sign here and report to Lieutenant Wingate; he'll swear you in. Then see Sergeant Tully; he'll issue you your gear and show you your quarters." So saying, he dipped the pen in the inkwell and offered it to Henry. Henry leaned over the desk and wrote "Henry", paused only a second, then added "Powell".

Henry made friends with another recruit named Roger Thornberry. Roger was a small man who gave his age as twenty-two and looked younger. He had delicate, almost feminine features with black hair and eyebrows.

The smallest uniform was too large for him and although from his appearance he seemed a far cry from a fighting man, if you took the trouble to look into the depth of his black eyes, you knew he was.

One evening as he and Henry were grooming their mounts, Roger confided that he had deserted the Union Army shortly after the battle of Fredericksburg. He then decided the best place to hide was back in the Army, so he had worked his way west with a wagon train and signed on at Fort Bent a couple of weeks before Henry arrived. Henry started to tell Roger what had caused him to leave Ohio, but he thought better of it and remained silent. It was the beginning of a strange friendship; one was a mountain of strength, the other had to strain to make the physical measurements of a grown man.

As far as the troopers were concerned, Roger and Henry were the errand boys for the company. They were accepted, but they had not been tested in battle and until they were they would merely be part of the trappings of L Troop.

The test came late in July when L Troop was deployed to seek and destroy a large band of Comanches under a renegade chief called Broken Hand. For six days, from dawn until dusk, they wound their way through the rugged country; across basins and up draws that finally led through narrow canyons into other basins, with still other mountains to pass over or through in the distance. Then, on the afternoon of the fifth day the men grew silent and Henry sensed that their instincts had forewarned them there would soon be action.

Lt. Wingate was a young officer, resplendent in his new uniform at the head of the column. Henry could see the crossed sabers on his shirt collar glistening in the sun from where he and Roger rode at the rear.

Sgt. Tully was a seasoned fighter and, like the rest of the troopers, he was dusty and dirty but comfortable that way. He took good care of Lt. Wingate, as he had the other young lieutenants before him, for it was a part of his job.

That night they made camp on the banks of a stream where the grass grew tall. When the campfire had been doused and the men were rolled into their blankets, Henry lay in the darkness looking up at the stars, thinking. He fell asleep wondering what lay ahead and how he would react in battle when it came. He would find out the next morning.

It was an Indian-screaming sunrise, with Comanches riding out of the east with the rising sun at their backs. They had a small element of surprise in their favor by coming in on the troopers' back trail. A heavy ring of sentries had been sent forward but only two covered the rear and there was little doubt that those two now had Comanche knives in their backs.

L Troop had been ready to mount and move out and Henry was at the far side of the camp when the attack took place. He had lugged a bag of farrier's tools toward the front of the column, where Corporal Kinnick was attending to a loose shoe on the Lieutenant's horse. Although Broken Hand led his warriors out of the draw at breakneck speed, L Troop reacted correctly at the first scream. The troopers were seasoned veterans for the most part and had been in surprise attacks before. Only three did not know what to do with themselves; Henry, Roger and the Lieutenant. None of them had ever seen a hundred screeching, charging Indians before. Sgt. Tully pulled the Lieutenant behind a rock and Corporal Kinnick shouted at Henry and Roger, "ON THE GROUND!"

In the meantime, the men had nullified any value the surprise attack might have had by acting courageously and without panic. Rifles were lifted from saddle scabbards and the men assigned to the horses gathered the reins and started them at a trot toward a nearby group of scrub pine. The other men sought cover as best they could, behind a rock, a bush, or kneeling in the tall grass, their Spencers firing with devastating accuracy. All this happened in only a few seconds, and by the time the charge had reached the outer edge of the camp the air was blue with gunsmoke and a half dozen Indians had been shot from their horses.

The front line of attackers carried the short, heavy Comanche lances which were hurled into the troopers from a distance of about twenty yards, then they wheeled aside as the main group charged ahead, firing rifles and arrows with little attempt to aim.

The troopers fought differently. They steadied their rifles, took aim, and squeezed off a shot only when they had centered their sights on a painted chest.

Broken Hand's hope for success was to charge into the camp and engage the troopers in hand-to-hand combat since the Indians outnumbered them two to one, but the men of L Troop did not intend to let that happen. They fired unhurriedly but accurately and Indian after Indian dropped to the ground.

Henry's emotions changed from fear to pride. During the first two or three seconds of the battle he had been sure they would all be killed and found himself fighting an almost overpowering urge to get up and run. But as he hugged the ground, listening to the steady crack of three dozen Spencers, he could tell that the shrieks of the charging Indians were beginning to wane. Finally, he risked raising his head just enough to watch the action. The Indians were still firing, but their forward movement had been stopped.

L Troop was not without casualties. Henry could see three crumpled troopers, one with an arrow protruding from his throat. Zeb, one of the men Henry had come to know, was kneeling just a little beyond and in front of Roger and was raising his rifle to his shoulder when a bullet struck him in the chest. Without a sound, Zeb toppled over and rolled onto his back. Almost immediately, Roger crawled along the ground to retrieve the fallen man's rifle. He raised himself to a kneeling position and was taking aim when the rifle flew out of his hand and he fell over backwards with blood streaming from his shoulder.

Henry spotted a puff of smoke in front of one of the braves at the instant Roger fell. The Indian had pulled off to the side and held his horse, intending to pick off as many troopers as he could. Henry slid forward and grabbed the rifle Roger had dropped. Still prone, he put the barrel across a rock, took sight dead center on the Comanche and squeezed the trigger. The brave slid off his horse and lay motionless on the ground; Henry had killed his first Indian. Almost as if that had been a signal, Broken Hand turned his band and rode back the way he had come.

The firing stopped and, one by one, the troopers stood up. Sgt. Tully took charge. "Corporal Kinnick," he called, "take a couple of men and tend to the wounded. Corporal Phillips, bring the Lieutenant a count on those dead Indians. Harrington, you take the south ridge and keep a close lookout. Anderson, take two men and scout the north flank. Becker, get the fire going and put some coffee on. Trooper Powell, you come with me."

Henry was trying to comfort Roger as the medic was cutting the uniform away from his wounded shoulder. "You'll be okay, buddy," he said and hurried after Sgt. Tully.

The Sergeant joined the Lieutenant and as Henry walked up he heard Sgt. Tully say, "Broken Hand is four or five days away from his main camp on the Platte. He can't take another whaling like we gave him today and he knows it. My thinking is he'll try to join up with Gray Horse. The scouts say about two hundred to two-fifty or so Ute braves led by Gray Horse are headin' north after raisin' hell down around Santa Fe. Now it's only a suggestion Lieutenant, but if I were you I'd get out a patrol to ride tail on Broken Hand and, bein's Broken Hand and Gray Horse make powwow, I'd mount this here troop and ride like Billy-be-damned for the fort."

The Lieutenant knew who was running L Troop, but he had to play his part as a strategy-trained officer. "Pick your patrol, Sergeant," he said.

"They'll be off within the hour, Lieutenant." Turning to Henry, he added, "Fetch four mounts and meet me back here in ten minutes."

A few minutes later, Henry and the Sergeant were riding toward the draw from which the Indian charge had materialized. Henry rode beside the Sergeant, holding the reins of the two extra horses.

"I was watchin' you today," the Sergeant spoke. "Just might be you'll make a fightin' man. You showed you got brains; a man lives longer when he knows how to think under fire. That's the kind of men I like in my outfit. Good work, Powell. Now, let's get on with our business." What that business was, Henry didn't know, but when the Sergeant spurred his horse, he followed.

They came upon the first sentry wedged between two rocks. The man was still alive, a feather-laden Comanche lance protruding from his stomach. As often as Sgt. Tully had witnessed the inhumanity of the Indians, he could not control his fury at the needless suffering of their victims; the spear could just as easily have been thrust into the man's chest and made his death a quick one. As it was, death was no less certain, but it would be agonizing hours in coming.

They tried to pour water into the doomed man's mouth, but he gurgled it away. "Take a good look," ordered the Sergeant. "Somewhere out there is a Comanche devil who did this thing and enjoyed every minute of it. They'll kill you, but they do it in such a way that you'll die a thousand times. So look real good, Trooper Powell. Let what you see pour into your eyes, fill your brain and run down into your guts so you'll never forget it."

Outwardly, Henry reacted very little, but in the presence of the dying man in that Godforsaken spot, he ceased being a boy.

The Sergeant knew that within seconds after he removed the shaft, merciful death would come. So, doing what had to be done, he grasped the shaft firmly with both hands, clenching his mind against the dreadful responsibility, and jerked it free. He cast the bloody pole aside, picked the man up and carried him to level ground. Taking the yellow handkerchief from his neck, he tied it across the man's face and knotted it at the back of his head. He unfastened his belt and crossed the man's hands at his waist, then tightened the belt over them and buckled it. "This is Trooper MacDonald," he said to Henry. "Secure his body to one of the horses, then we'll look for Leaderman. He's likely in that clump of mesquite at the end of the draw and you can be sure they had their sport with him, too. Let's hope he's dead, but likely he ain't."

They found George Leaderman lashed to the trunk of a mesquite tree in a half-sitting position, an arrow buried in his left shoulder and one in each thigh. He had been scalped and viciously slashed across the face. His right hand had been severed.

Sgt. Tully cut the rope and lowered the wounded trooper to the ground. Henry stood behind him, looking down at the bloody, mutilated figure. In God's name, what can we do for the man? he wondered. Finally, his senses could stand no more and he walked off a few paces. Moments later, he watched as the Sergeant walked to his horse and began to fumble with his saddle roll. He removed a revolver and walked back, dropping it beside Leaderman.

The sound of the shot ripped at Henry's already shattered nerves. He looked back in time to see the service revolver slip from Leaderman's hand; he had put a bullet in his temple. "You knew he was going to do that when you walked away! How could you..." Henry shouted.

The Sergeant's eyes were blazing. "What the hell would you have done, you green-necked kid? You think this is a hayride we're on? You tangle with one of these red bastards some day and you may beg someone to blow your brains out. Now shut your damn mouth and keep it shut! Get that man on a horse and let's get the hell outta here!"

Henry did as he was told and they rode off. Three quarters of an hour later, the burial detail finished its work near an outcropping of rock and five mounds of dirt were recorded with X's on the official map to be filed at headquarters when they got back.

Henry checked on his friend Roger and learned he would recover. He then sought Sgt. Tully. "Sergeant, sir..." he began.

"How the hell many times have I told you not to call me 'sir'," the Sergeant bellowed. "What's on your mind?"

"I'd like to be assigned to that patrol I heard you tell the Lieutenant about."

"Job like that takes experienced men, Powell." The Sergeant stopped and studied Henry's face. "Well, 'pears you might have a little bile in your mouth at that. It's called Injun hatred. Time'll come when you can spit pure poison just at the thought of a redskin. Might be the time is right for you to get a little experience. Report to Corporal Kinnick."

"Thank you sir...I mean, Sergeant."

Henry told the Corporal he was there under the Sergeant's orders. The man's sour look was not one of welcome, but he offered no comment.

"Listen, men," he said. "I want you to strip everything that makes the slightest sound or anything that shines or can be seen from a distance. You'll not be riding your reg'lar mounts. I've picked five of the fastest horses in the comp'ny. Each man will have a canteen, a handful of biscuits, his rifle and what rounds the magazine'll hold. We're gonna shadow Broken Hand, so all my orders will be hand signals. If he crosses trail with Gray Horse, Red Cloud or any other band, our job is to get the message back to the Lieutenant pronto. There'll be no time to stop and fight. All we do is ride and hope some of us gits back. Are there any questions?"

The sun was dead center overhead when the patrol rode out. The following evening, two of them rode back and the troopers of L Company gathered to meet them. Corporal Kinnick lay forward over his horse's neck, seriously wounded. Henry Powell sat erect, in a daze. His arms, chest and back were a series of gashes and he was drenched with blood. They were placed on blankets and Henry stared into space while his wounds were tended.

Corporal Kinnick held his hand over the knife wound in his midsection as Sgt. Tully built him a smoke and the Lieutenant raised his head so one of the men could give him a drink from a canteen. He drank, coughed blood, then drank again. He began to talk. "You never saw anything like it," he gasped. "Private Powell fought like a demon from hell. We stopped in a draw and I sent a man on foot to scout the ridge. He was barely halfway up when they hit us. There was a good two dozen, Lieutenant, and they came over the edge of the draw from all directions. Murphy and Tennbrock went down right away. Moore, who was afoot, got a couple and Powell and I each got a couple more before they got too close for us to use our rifles. Then the red hellions slid off their ponies and came at us with knives.

"For a while, Powell and I were back to back. When I felt that Comanche blade go in my brisket, I was sure we'd had it, but I guess the knife went in a little low. Such a fight you would never believe. Powell took his rifle by the barrel and was bashing redskins right and left. Every time the butt landed I could hear bones crunch. When one got close enough to swipe with his knife, Henry'd grab the redskin's arm and snapped it like a twig. He swung his rifle with his right hand and clubbed skulls with his left. Whenever a knife got to him, he swung that mighty fist and the Indian dropped. He kicked and punched and whaled with that rifle butt 'til he stood in a circle of dead an' dyin' Indians. It was a sight to wait a lifetime for. It sure grieves me that I won't be the one to tell the story come gab-time in the barracks.

"Finally, though, the three hostiles left jumped on their ponies and took out over the ridge. Goin' to Broken hand for help, I figured, so Henry and me lit out for camp. I wouldn'ta believed it, Lieutenant, if I hadn't seen it." Glancing over at Henry lying next to him, he added, "Yessir, you got yourself one helluva soldier in that man."

Sgt. Tully put a lighted cigarette between the Corporal's lips. He took a deep puff and closed his eyes.

The story the Corporal told was being told again at that moment in the camp of Gray Horse. Talks In The Night, half brother to Gray Horse, was one of the two comanches who had escaped to tell of the terrible slaughter of his brothers by a single cavalryman. As he related his incredible tale, Henry Powell earned a new name among the Comanche: Buffalo Walks Like A Man. Indians admired courage and strength, so the story was carried on the smoke from the camps of the Comanche to the Cheyenne, from the Sioux to the Crow, from the Blackfeet to the Ute.

In future engagements with the Indians at Sandy Creek, Dead Dog Mesa, Turtle Wells and Bonito Springs, Henry fought with the strength and truculence of ten men and his legend grew. Even the great chiefs, Crazy Horse, Two Moons and Spotted Tail came to listen with stoic admiration to the exploits of the trooper known as Buffalo Walks Like A Man.

In the meantime, however, the wounded Henry Powell was being prepared for the trip back to Fort Bent. Corporal Kinnick had fooled everyone. The moon had made half its nocturnal trip and he still lived. The flow of blood had been stopped and the wound packed.
"He's a tough soldier. He might just make it," Sgt. Tully commented.
A bed was made in a supply wagon for the Corporal and preparations began for the long trip back to the fort. Roger's shoulder had been dressed and bandaged and he would return as he had come, in the saddle. Henry's cuts were not serious, but they burned as if he had been seared with a branding iron.
Henry kneed his mount and fell in beside Roger. He glanced at his small friend, who said, "Damned if I don't hear you went and made a hero of yourself."
"Just a rumor," Henry replied. "Pay it no mind." And the two recruits of a few days ago headed for home, seasoned veterans.
Henry was awarded a citation for bravery in due time and within six months he made corporal. A year later, Sgt. Granville Tully's scalp decorated the doorway of a Cheyenne teepee and Henry became Sgt. Powell. Engagements with the Indians were frequent for a while, then they left the warpath and could not be found. Life at the fort became routine until one day many months later when a company of men were ordered to join Captain Keogh at Fort Phil Kearny in Wyoming, there to await further orders.
The orders from Washington read, "...you are therefore to dispatch without delay a full company of your best fighting men, complete with all necessary supplies and ammunition, to take part in a full-scale campaign under the command of Lieutenant General George Custer."
L Troop was the first to move out. Lt. Wingate left the Commander's office and told Sgt. Powell to have his men ready to leave in two hours.
"What's happening, Lieutenant?" Henry questioned.

"Temporary reassignment, Sergeant. We're heading north to Fort Phil Kearny to rendezvous with the Seventh at the Rosebud. Have the men check their gear and weapons and replace anything worn or broken. I want this outfit in top shape."

"Must have a real butt-buster comin' up," Henry observed.

"The whole Sioux nation, I hear, with the Cheyenne, the Crow and a few other tribes thrown in!"

"That'll be a right lively tussle. Who's headin' up this shindig?" Henry asked.

"General Custer to you and me, Yellow Hair to Crazy Horse and his Sioux. Get a move on, Sergeant, time's running out."

Sgt. Powell had never mastered the art of saluting but he gave it his best effort and started for the barracks.

"Sergeant," the Lieutenant called. "Sergeant Tully took a painted feather off the body of Little Crow that day at Bonito Springs. Do you know what became of it?"

"Yessir, Lieutenant, the supply sergeant has it."

"Bring it to me," the Lieutenant commanded.

Capt. Keogh was waiting at Fort Phil Kearny, which was bulging with men. The Lieutenant was informed that his men were to be given one hour to eat, clean up and be on the parade ground. In less than an hour Henry had them at attention and in their assigned spaces.

There was little doubt in the minds of the hundreds of men assembled that the officer who rode up and down the lines on a tour of inspection was Captain Keogh. As he passed, Henry saw a man with a stern countenance, sweeping gray eyes and a moustache that drooped over the corners of his mouth. Minutes later, facing the men without dismounting, he spoke in a voice that carried to every corner of the compound.

"I have been told that you are hand-picked men, the pride of the U.S. Cavalry. That's good. You've been brought here to join forces with my men and the men under the commands of Captain Benteen and General Custer. We are going after the Sioux, who are led by the greatest military strategist of the Indian Nations, Crazy Horse. He has been joined by the Cheyenne in great numbers and they are led by Dull Knife, Spotted Calf, Two Moons and Sitting Bull. Our scouts tell us other tribes are on the way to join them."

"Our job is to seek out Crazy Horse and his warriors and defeat them before the other tribes are organized. We will be engaging the finest warriors of the Sioux nation in the greatest numbers ever brought together under one chief and it will be a fight to the death for Crazy Horse will never surrender."

"I've instructed your lieutenants to split their companies to assure equal strength among General Custer, Captain Benteen and myself. We will leave the fort an hour before sunrise. My compliments to your officers and the best of luck to you all."

While they were still in formation, Lt. Wingate divided L Troop. Henry missed the contingent assigned to General Custer and was the first one named in the group slated for Captain Benteen. He had hoped to be assigned to Custer and he was doubly disappointed when Lt. Wingate placed himself with the Custer detachment.

It was a long, two-day ride. There was no singing to break the monotony, none of the usual bantering or horesplay. Only the squeaking of leather and the clopping of hoofs accompanied the troopers, along with the heat and the choking, yellow dust. Henry tried to estimate the number of men in the long line that draped itself over the rolling land like a long, blue snake. Three hundred or more, he was sure, and mostly strangers. He missed the security of L Troop.

They made camp at sunset and since no fires were allowed, the evening meal consisted of dried beef and biscuits, washed down with warm water from their canteens. After caring for their mounts, they rolled into their blankets to sleep. Swarms of mosquitoes hung over the camp, singing above their heads and stabbing exposed flesh. Slaps, groans and curses rippled across the circle of tired men.

Each man was awakened the next morning with the toe of a boot. No bugles, no fires; it was biscuits and water and into the saddle. The second day was a repeat of the first; heat, dust and sweat and endless hours of riding.

Henry had struck up an acquaintance with the trooper riding next to him, one Christian Reibold from Virginia. He was stationed at Fort Benton and had been assigned to Custer's company. Henry tried to arrange a swap, but to no avail. The trooper felt, as most of the men did, that if a big Indian battle was coming up, the safest place to ride was behind the greatest Indian fighter of them all, Lt. General George Armstrong Custer.

Toward evening Henry could see a line of green foliage covering the trail ahead and he mentioned it to Christian. "That's a line of willows, Look off to your right. See that large clump of trees? According to the Major, that's where the Tongue joins the Rosebud. If you look close you can see an encampment of cavalrymen; that'll be Custer and the Seventh."

A sergeant and two corporals rode out to meet them and as the men passed by they were directed by arm signals to the command for which they had been chosen, Keogh, Benteen or Custer.

During the evening Henry kept a sharp eye out for a glimpse of General Custer and he also looked for Roger. On his way back to his blankets, he picked up snatches of conversation as he walked along.

"..Johnson said the Corporal told him there was ten thousand Indians west of.."

"... said Crazy Horse has the whole damn Sioux nation waitin' for..."

"...Curly, Custer's scout, says there's Uncapapas, Minneconjous, Cheyenne, Blackfeet and..."

"...did it at the Washita and he'll do it again no matter.."

Henry passed an old veteran who was staring across the Rosebud to the west. His words were low, but Henry caught them. "Rest, Crazy Horse, but a little while. You'll meet Yellow Hair come tomorrow."
Henry smiled and walked on. He reached for his plug of tobacco and bit off a big chew. What in tarnation have I got myself into? he thought. Crazy Horse? Sitting Bull? Ten thousand indians? "Whoee," he muttered. "Don't exactly sound like a chivaree they got planned. 'Low as how I better look to my gear before mornin'." He spent

the last fifteen minutes before turning in putting the stone to his sheath knife, spitting and honing until the edge glistened with sharpness and the blade was brown with tobacco juice. It would be red with Sioux blood before the next sunset.

To the men who fought there, red and white, it was the Battle of the Greasy Grass. Those who talked about it later named it the Battle of the Little Big Horn.

The Little Big Horn River is barely as wide as a man is tall. It wanders as silently and peacefully through the grasslands of Montana as a field mouse scampering in play. You would scarcely know it was there if it were not for the brush and small trees that grow along its banks; a most unlikely place for the cataclysmic clash of red and white man that took place in the bright sunlight of June 25, 1876.

During the early morning hours the men were roused and told to saddle up. They were told to leave everything but their carbines, revolvers and ammunition, and there was to be no talking or unnecessary noise. Custer's scouts had reported seeing a large Sioux village on the banks of the Little Big Horn and his plan was to strike immediately and catch them by surprise, as he had done at the Washita.

The great body of soldiers moved through the night like stalking wolves. During the false dawn they halted in a draw and the officers met in consultation with Custer. Henry steadied his restless bay and got his first look at the leader of the famous Seventh Cavalry.

Custer was dressed in buckskin and looked much younger than Henry expected. He wore a light brown, wide-brimmed hat with one side of brim fastened to the crown. His skin-tight boots reached above the knee and two pearl-handled revolvers swung at his hips. But his most striking feature, and what made him well known to all the tribes of the Plains Indian was the carefully dressed, long yellow hair that fell to his collar.

There appeared to be a heated discussion among the officers, but the matter was quickly settled for suddenly Custer reined his horse and rode to his troops. Captain

Benteen raced his horse toward his command and came to a rearing stop, calling out, "Sergeant Stanley, Sergeant Powell, front!"

With a little surprise that his name was known, Henry spurred his horse to the head of the column. Capt. Benteen's face was flushed and his words came fast.

"The General has ordered us to charge the village. His scouts report that we've been spotted. Sergeant Stanley, order the bugler to sound Charge."

The men were keyed up and itching for a fight. The minute they recognized the bugler's call, a hundred yells split the morning silence and at the second leap they were in full gallop. As they rode by the rear of Custer's command, Henry passed within ten feet of Roger. They exchanged a wave and then Henry was gone.

George Armstrong Custer, Lieutenant General in the United States Cavalry, Indian fighter and glory hunter, moved out at a trot onto the dark ridge that paralleled the Little Big Horn and two hundred and fifty-five loyal and trusting men followed him into the pages of history. One hour and twenty minutes later, on a knoll at the end of the ridge, the guidons carrying the large red "7" would be lying among the bodies of Custer and his entire company until a warrior on a painted pony swept it from the ground and raced with it toward the Indian village on the banks of the Little Big Horn River.

In the distance, nearly two thousand screaming Sioux, having completed the slaughter of the Seventh Cavalry, rode back across the Little Big Horn and engaged Captain Benteen.

On the knoll with Custer, Trooper Roger Thornberry had been one of the first to die. A Cheyenne buffalo lance buried itself deep in his chest while he was still in the saddle and he fell at the very instant that Custer shouted the order to dismount.

Lt. Wingate was one of the last. A rifle slug smacked into his temple and he fell at Custer's feet. He had placed the feather Sgt. Tully had taken from Little Crow in the band of his hat. A member of the burial crew found it the next day and slipped it into his own hatband.

General Custer bled his life away with his head cradled in the lap of one of his mortally wounded men. When the guidons of the seventh went down for the last time, a silence settled over the knoll while the wind wept.

Captain Benteen's charge ran into a screeching red wall. The front ranks of his men were falling from their saddles with terrifying frequency as the troopers fired into the mass of Indians facing them as fast as they could lever rounds into the chambers. Their rifles overheated and jammed and were cast aside, and they drew their revolvers and continued firing. It was a losing battle and Benteen knew it. He rode among the men and shouted, "Back to the river! Into the trees!"

Along the bank of the Little Big Horn, the men dismounted and were able to direct a withering fire into the milling hostiles from the cover of the trees. Throughout the afternoon the battle raged as they repulsed charge after charge. Many men died and many more were wounded, but as the day wore on it appeared that the troopers could hold out.

However, toward evening the Indians massed for another charge. Led by Chief Gall, they broke for Benteen's position and even though the troopers' bullets thudded into a hundred bare chests, the momentum carried a few warriors into the ranks of the exhausted soldiers. Those who made it were quickly cut down, but not before they had caused additional dead and wounded among the troopers.

Henry was keeping a close watch on Captain Benteen. A brave who was pulled from his horse killed the trooper who had dragged him down, then leveled his rifle at the Captain. Henry saw it and threw himself at the Indian, and in so doing took a slug that shattered his hip and ended his military career. A second later Henry slid the blade of his knife between the ribs of the Sioux brave and drew it out, red with blood. Captain Benteen's back was turned while his attention was centered elsewhere and he did not see Henry's sacrifice, nor did Henry ever tell him.

The Indians withdrew as darkness settled in and attention was given to the wounded. Captain Benteen made the rounds, them stopped to talk with Henry. "They tell me you're going to be fine, Sergeant," he said.

"I'll make it all right, Cap'n," Henry replied.

The officer put his hand on Henry's shoulder. "Sure you will, son. Just you lie quiet."

Henry smiled. He was so full of belladonna that he was drowsy and had trouble focusing his eyes.

"General Terry is due tomorrow morning," he heard the Captain continue, "and I'm sure the Indian scouts have reported his approach to Crazy Horse and Sitting Bull. If we can hold out till dark we'll all make it."

It remained quiet along the banks of the Greasy Grass. The sun settled into the tall buffalo grass and soon the men could see the reflections of stars in the black surface of the little river. Sitting Bull's scouts had indeed informed him of the approach of General Terry and his troops, and he had directed the various tribes to slip off into the night. Far off a coyote barked, then there was silence.

The gentle fingers of the evening breeze touched the cheeks of the living and the dead alike, Custer as he slept and Bentine as he watched over his troops. Darkness covered the land and the fearful battle of the Little Big Horn was over.

The wounded were transported to Fort Phil Kearny and Henry spent three weeks there, alternating between a consciousness filled with pain and hallucinations spawned by delirium. But, finally, he began to heal and the fever passed and he joined the other walking wounded in their morning exercise. The men seldom talked, preferring to be alone with their thoughts but whenever conversation sprang up, it was about the battle along the Greasy Grass. That was how Henry learned that General Custer and his entire detachment had been killed. He thought of his friend Roger and of Capt. Keogh and wondered how they died.

On the morning of August first, a small caravan of five ambulances, escorted by what remained of L Troop, headed home to Fort Bent. It was a slow and painful journey. Life slipped away from two of the most seriously wounded troopers and they were buried along the trail; two graves unmarked and unknown, two men to be honored in the memories of those who fought beside them on that terrible afternoon near the Little Big Horn River.

CHAPTER TEN
Toward Buell

As the days went by, Frank spent more of his time in the Nugget Saloon. Doc Hathaway had treated Jed's wounds and Frank was the first to greet him when he returned to work some weeks later, the stump of his right wrist still swathed in bandages.

Before long Jed realized that Frank was trying to hide in a bottle. During their many talks Jed was able to convince Frank that his life had to go on, that he could not turn back the clock or ward off the furture with liquor. "Your dad was mighty proud of you Frank, and you got no justification to drown yourself in booze like you are."

"I could have saved Pa that night Jed, and you know it."

"Maybe so and maybe not, but there ain't no use stewin' about it the rest of your life. You can't change it so you gotta accept it and go on living the best you know how. That girl of yours Frank, you're mighty lucky to have her, but you're gonna lose her, too, if you keep on like this. You owe it to her to be the man she thought you were when she said she'd marry you. Hell's fire, boy, you ain't the only one in the world that's ever been gully-drug." He held up the stub of his right hand.

Frank stood lost in thought for awhile then turned and walked out, leaving a glass of whiskey on the bar.

After a June wedding, Frank and Opal moved into the house he had shared with his father and he gradually returned to the good-natured young man he had been before his father's death. He went to work for Abe Sloan in the Carson City Bank for five dollars a week, with the promise of a fifty-cent raise at the end of the year. Shortly after he started his new job, Opal told him he would be a father in early spring. Suddenly, life took a new turn.

Opal delighted in keeping house for Frank, and Frank enjoyed the respect the townspeople showed him because of his job at the bank. Life went singing along for the Applegates. A baby girl arrived in May and they named her Nan.

They had a scare the first winter when she became sick. Her cries awakened Opal in the middle of the night and she aroused Frank. He ran, half dressed, all the way to Doc Hathaway's office. An hour later, with a reassuring smile and a pat on Opal's shoulder, he said, "Little Nan has chickenpox. Keep her warm and give her this in small doses." He handed Opal a peppermint stick.

At noon a few months later, Frank came bursting into the house with news. "I've been promoted to cashier!"

Opal threw her arms around his neck and kissed him. "Darling, that's wonderful! I'm very proud of you!"

Frank picked Nan up in his arms. "Young lady, your pa's comin' up in the world," he said. Nan responded by banging him on the nose with her rag doll.

"Now, Mister New Cashier, I have some news for you. You're going to be a father again!" Opal announced.

Frank stared at her a moment, then broke into a broad smile. "The trouble with this family is, they can't do things one at a time. Everything comes in bunches." Opal's news called for another kiss and an embrace and this time it lasted a little longer.

A week after Tommy was born, Frank and Opal bought the Stevenson's Dry Goods Store. Frank had learned at the bank that Charlie Stevenson intended to sell and from the price quoted, he decided it would be a fine deal. He checked their savings and found they had almost enough to make the down payment.

When he went home for lunch that day, he told Opal about his idea. "I don't see how we can pass it up. If I can borrow a little from the bank we can swing it. The store'd give us a good living for the rest of our lives and, as proprietors, we'd have a fine standing in the community. It's almost a sure thing that we could save enough money to send the children to one of those Eastern colleges."

He glanced at Opal to see how she was taking it. She was biting her lower lip, as she always did whenever she was in deep thought. "Another thing," he continued, "you and the children could have all the clothes and yard goods you needed and it wouldn't cost a penny. Of course, it'd take us a while to pay off Mister Stevenson and business might go bad for some reason..."

"Frank," she interrupted, "let's buy it."

Frank worked hard at being a storekeeper. He had much to learn about merchandising and the lamp in his office burned late many a night as he struggled over order forms and profit and loss journals. He ran a tidy store, greeted his customers with a smile and special-ordered anything he did not have in stock. Business was good and at the end of the first year he was able to pay Mr. Stevenson twice the amount they had agreed upon.

Midway into his second year, he contracted to buy the Black and Haines Harness and Buggy Shop next door. In November, he was elected alderman. He came home from the meeting that night to catch Opal with flour on her nose in a kitchen smelling of freshly-baked bread.

"I bear great news, Missus Applegate," he announced from the doorway. "You are now the wife of a Carson City alderman." He opened his arms and she rushed into them. After a pride-filled kiss and an extra tight embrace, she pushed away and took a step back. Frank caught the familiar gleam in her eye. "Oh no!" he said. "You're not going to top me again?"

With an impish grin, she nodded.

No one ever knew for sure how the fire started, but the Nugget Saloon was the first to go. After supper Frank and little Tommy had gone back to the store, where Frank intended to work on invoices. He had been at his desk about a half an hour when he heard a commotion and loud voices next door. He went outside and saw that the rear of the saloon, only a few feet from his building, was burning fiercely. Even as he watched, the flame crept across the roof of the Nugget. A crowd was gathering and Frank heard the horse-drawn pumper approaching. One look at the flames, now climbing into the heavens, made him realize that the Nugget and his own building were doomed.

He had ordered heavily for the winter season and

every penny he had in the world was just minutes away from going up in smoke. He plunged into the crowd and pleaded for assistance to help him save what he could of his merchandise. "They'll never stop this thing," he shouted. "When they pump the watering troughs dry, they're finished. I need help with the store!"

Several men responded and he ran with them into his store. He yelled for them to grab an armful of whatever they could and stack it across the street. One of the men was Jed, the bartender of the Nugget. "My place is a goner," he said, "but maybe we can save yours."

They worked feverishly, making trip after trip on a dead run and the pile of pants, shoes, yard goods and sundries began to grow.

The building on the other side of the Nugget was now burning. The fire created its own whirlwind, which whipped the embers of the Nugget, casting a red glow into the street like the main chambers of Hell. The intense heat had driven the onlookers backward to the edge of darkness. Frank stopped in the street to appraise the situation and saw that the roof of his store was in flames. He knew the men could only make one or two more trips safely. He had started for the front door again when Opal grabbed him by the arm.

"Frank," she screamed above the roar of the flames, "where's Tommy?"

The cold hand of fear clutched at Frank's heart at her words and almost stopped its beating. Tommy! Frank had heard him playing on the second floor where the Christmas toys were stored while he was working, and in the excitement he had forgotten the boy! He glanced up at the second story window, but seeing no sign of his son he gathered his strength and began to run. When he reached the stairway that led to the upper level, the heat and thick smoke cut at his throat and lungs like thousands of tiny blades; the upper half of the stairway was in flames.

Draught between the two floors acted like a bellows and each time he started up, the fire ballooned down and drove him back. Fear of the fire and fear for his son waged a battle within him that nearly destroyed his sanity. Whether the words were spoken only in his heart or whether he actually heard them he would never know, but he would hear them in his soul for the rest of his life: "Daddy! Daddy!"

Wracked with sobs, he started up the stairs, but, again, a sheet of flame billowed around him. He backed down once more and stood shaking as the torment of conflict ripped through him. He was still standing there seconds later when Jed brushed by him, charged the stairs and returned through the wall of flames carrying Tommy. Jed pushed Frank ahead of him and the three of them rushed into the street. Jed's and Tommy's clothes were burning, but the flames were quickly extinguished when some of the onlookers wrapped them in blankets. Their exposed skin was blackened and blistered. Jed placed the boy on a pile of blankets among the salvaged merchandise.

Opal was almost in hysterics and was restrained by two of the women until Doc Hathaway could examine the boy. Frank stood to one side, trembling and dazed. When the doctor finally stood up, Frank walked over to him.

"I'm sorry, Frank. If we'd only been a few seconds sooner..."

Frank lowered his face into his hands and dropped to his knees in the street. The leaping flames of the burning store behind him caused his shadow to writhe and tumble in the agony that possessed his body. The small piece of self-respect left to him curled and hardened within his mind and the sharp edges cut into his soul.

Tommy was buried next to his grandfather and, again, it was Opal's strength that carried Frank through. Their neighbors and close friends escorted them home. Opal felt an emptiness in her as big as Tommy's grave, but her healing began when she felt the coming child move within her body.

One afternoon shortly thereafter, Frank walked to the pile of ashes and charred timbers that had once been his store. He stared at the ruins and the horrible moments at the foot of the stairs came back to him. Again he heard the voice of his son and the damning words of Doc Hathaway: "If we'd only been a few seconds sooner!"

His cowardice, exposed in the blazing inferno, was know only to himself and Jed, but it had cost the life of his son and how in God's name could he ever find relief from the torment of that knowledge! Frank's thoughts were as black and desolate as the destruction that lay before him. He finally turned and walked the few doors west to a storeroom where, with the help of some planks and barrels, the Nugget had gone back in business.

Jed was at home nursing his burns and the owner, O.E. Paulson, was pouring drinks at the makeshift bar. Frank went home late that night, drunk and foul-tempered and he stayed drunk for so many days that Opal lost count. Sometimes he drank at the saloon and sometimes at home. A few times he was seen standing ankle-deep in the ashes of the store, one hand clutching an open bottle, the other balled into a fist as he hurled drunken curses heavenward. One day, Reverend Hetherington entered the church and found Frank sitting alone in a back pew, his cheeks wet with tears and his hands clasped in prayer.

One cool morning in early autumn Frank's drinking came to an end. He had burned out some of the anger and frustration that had imprisoned his mind and what was left was as gray and lifeless as the pile of ashes down the street. He was barely aware of the discomfort of his hangover and spent his time sitting in a chair in the parlor staring through the window, seeing nothing and saying nothing. He made no response to statements for question from Opal. At night he slept fitfully, often getting up and sitting in his chair to stare into the night.

After three or four days of this, Opal could not stand it any longer, so one evening she lit a lamp and placed it on the fireplace mantel near Frank, then knelt by his side. "Frank, the baby is due soon and I need you. Please darling, won't you come back to me?" she pleaded.

Frank turned and looked for a long time into the imploring eyes of his wife and gradually began to return from some faraway land of oblivion. He became aware again and his love for her sparked compassion in his heart, showing in the look of tenderness that stole over his face. He pulled Opal to him and their kiss was flavored with the salt of their tears.

The next morning, Frank displayed some degree of normalcy. "I believe I'll take inventory today of what we were able to save from the fire," he said.

Opal smiled her approval, "By the way, I had old Joe next door cover it with canvas," she told him.

While Frank was busy sorting and itemizing the merchandise, a horse and buggy pulled up beside him and Nick Gleason, the jobber for Honkwiler and Hobson, Wholesalers, stepped down. "Frank," he began, "I just got the story of what happened. I can't tell you how sorry I am. Is there anything I can do?"

Frank looked hard at the city-dressed salesman with his tie and stickpin, blue suit and dust-sprinkled shoeshine. Little man, he thought, if you were ten feet tall and had a bolt of lightning in one hand and a bar of gold in the other, there wouldn't be one damn thing you could do for me. What he said was, "Nope, I reckon not."

"I'm sure I can get my company to back you. You've been a good customer, always paid in full and on time, so find another building and we'll get you started back in business."

They were the first thoughts about the future that had registered in Frank's mind since the fire. He stood for a long time, lost in thought, then, without a word to his visitor, he flipped the canvas back over the dry goods and headed for home with long, rapid strides. He found Opal making the beds. "We're leaving Carson City," he announced.

He left Opal looking bewildered and hurried out of the Nugget. He had a sudden desire to talk to Jed. With a tall mug of beer in his hand, he made his announcement to his friend. "We're pulling out of Carson City."

Jed looked up sharply and paused for a moment to think about Frank's words, then he went back to polishing glasses. Frank finished his beer and pushed the glass toward Jed.

"Well, ain't you gonna say somethin'?"
"It's a funny thing, Frank," Jed answered, "but I been thinkin' of that very thing myself."

"That's great! We'll go together!" Frank exclaimed.
"Where'll we go?" Jed asked.

"Oh hell, I don't know, somewhere, anywhere. There must be a town in the Territory someplace that can use a general store."

"I know of a town." The words came from Nick Gleason who had been taking in the conversation from a nearby table. He joined Frank at the bar and they listened to what he had to say.

That night at supper, Frank told Opal again that they were leaving Carson City. "I got to," he said. "I just plain sure as hell got to. So, soon as the baby arrives and you're able to travel we'll be movin' out. By the way, Jed's going with us. He feels like me...he can't get the smell of smoke out of his nose. Nick Gleason told us of a mining town that's beginning to boom, but it has no general store."

"Where is it?" Opal asked.

"In the Arizona Territory, southeast of Tucson a piece; a town named Buell."

CHAPTER ELEVEN
Angeline

Sgt. Henry Powell was mustered out of the United State Cavalry on December 20, 1876. It was apparent even to Henry that his injury made him unfit for duty and he was only one of many whose wounds had left them unsuitable for service. All the others chose to leave the fort, some to return home and spend the rest of their days as invalids, the rest to seek a new life in other fields.

Henry alone elected to stay since he could not return home and he had lost his desire for California. General Miles accepted his request for civilian employment and he went to work in the blacksmith shop. He worked hard and talked little, but his consumption of the settler's whiskey soon became the talk of the fort. He aged beyond his years--he was barely twenty-five--and became know as "Old Sarge" among the younger troopers.

As the weeks rolled by Henry became sullen and morose. He spent his time slamming a large hammer against a white-hot piece of steel lying across the anvil, or pounding nails through a shoe into the hoofs of countless horses. And with each pause of his arm he would send a gusher of tobacco juice against the base of the forge. Each morning and each evening he bought a bottle of rye at the sutlers and within an hour the bottle was empty.

Henry was aware of the departure of L Troop from time to time and of the many vacant saddles when they returned. He spotted the recruits by their new blue uniforms, but in general he paid very little attention to the activities of the fort. He worked and drank and it appeared that this would be the life of ex-Sgt. Henry Powell. But destiny had a role for him to play in the faraway town of Buell, Arizona, and the first event to take him there occurred in midafternoon of a February day in 1877. A group of troopers on a routine patrol had spotted a small wagon train under Indian attack some eight miles north of Fort Bent. A messenger galloped into the compound early in the morning with a request for help and a detachment was sent out immediately. They returned with the survivors and among them was Miss Angeline Patton.

Angeline was every inch a lovely woman. She was tall and carried herself with a regal air that commanded attention. Her glistening black hair was braided and looped into two coils tightly pinned at the back of her head. Her eyes were dark brown beneath heavy, arched brows. She presented a classic loveliness never before seen at Fort Bent.

She had come to see the commanding officer to demand that the savages who had attacked their train be brought in and punished. Upon her request, a trooper had been sent to escort her to headquarters and they were walking now along a path that took them by the blacksmith's shop. As they passed, Henry was nailing on a shoe and he chose that moment to lift his head and let go with a long stream of tobacco juice; most of it landed on the lady's gown about knee high and that was how Henry Powell met Angeline Patton.

    Angeline looked down at her dress in disbelief, than looked up at Henry and began berating him with the most uncomplimentary adjectives he had ever heard from a female. He let the hammer slip from his grasp and straightened to his full height. As the words pelted him, he gazed at the beauty of the angry girl before him and for the first time in many a day he smiled broadly.

    "You've ruined my dress! Well, sir, what are you going to do about it?" she stormed.

    The two stood looking at each other for a few seconds in silence. Then Henry's heart spoke to his mind. He had to have this beautiful woman! "I'm going to marry you," was his astonishing reply.

    And marry her he did, after two months of persistent and passionate courting. There was a big celebration at the fort with the regimental band furnishing the music for a square dance. There was food and drink, laughter and dancing, and Henry was almost his old self. He even took a soap and water bath and shaved, combed his hair, and dug out and pressed his old uniform.

The wedding was performed by the commanding officer and L Troop lined up to kiss the bride until Henry objected. "Hold it, fellas. My wife can't kiss the entire U.S. Cavalry," he said good naturedly.

This announcement was followed by a chorus of moans and groans. Angeline brought smiles to their faces, however, when she overruled her new husband and directed L Troop to line up in columns of two in front of her. Bending forward slightly, she thrust our her pretty face for the troopers to kiss, one man on each cheek. The ceremony was followed by three cheers for the bride and groom and the evening was over.

Henry's and Angeline's happiness in their two rooms in civilian quarters was short-lived. Every time troopers left the Fort on patrol Henry was inconsolable and his temper flared with increasing regularity, his periods of moody silence becoming longer and more frequent. He drank as steadily as he breathed and at night he paced the floor for hours in his restlessness.

Angeline truly loved the brute of a man she had married, so she decided they should leave Fort Bent to see if he could find peace in the mountains and plains of the free country to the west. It took some talking and waiting, but she finally convinced him to go.

On the morning they left, the first warm winds of spring moved in and Angeline noticed with a pang of regret that the green shoots were just peeking through in the flower box under her window. They were leaving before reveille to avoid the goodbyes Henry so heartily disliked. The evening before, he had had a talk with the General, cleared his departure with the Captain of the Guard, and loaded all their possessions into the wagon provided him by General Miles, so that it was only a matter of hitching the team to the wagon and tying his Appaloosa to the tailgate this morning.

The quiet and darkness in the great enclosure of the Fort drew into the outer edges of the light from Henry's lantern. The muffled steps of the sentries were the only sounds to be heard. Henry helped Angeline up to the seat, shoved his carbine into the boot and climbed in beside her. He clucked to the team and they were on their way. As they passed through the large gate the guard came to attention, saluted and called out, "Good luck,

Sarge!" Angeline clasped her husband's arm and snuggled close to him, smiling her contentment.

The land that lay ahead of them was as black as the sky above. The wagon bumped and creaked and Henry let the horses set their own pace. They were in no hurry for they did not know how far they were going, nor where.

After a few miles, Henry began to feel the first touches of excitement about his wife's plan. "Angie," he said, "what do you reckon we're doin' out here in the middle o' the boonies, smack-dab in the center of Indian country and headed for God only knows where?" When Angeline did not answer at once, he continued, "We must be plumb out of our minds. How did you ever get such an idea, anyway?"

"Something had to be done, Henry. I just felt that if we could get some things straightened out."

"What things?" Henry asked.

"The things you have inside you that won't let you rest, that torment you and make you miserable. You're a bothered man, Henry Powell, and whatever's bothering you we're going to bring out in the open. Then I'm going to fill the inside of you with so much love there'll be no hiding places left. When the day comes I've done that, we'll stop this wagon and our journey will be over."

"Why, I hardly know anything about you, Henry. I want to know about your boyhood and your folks and your dog, if you had one. I want to know about your dreams and your plans, and I want to know what you want to do with your life because I'm a big part of it now. So start talking, Mister Powell." They rode a while in silence and Angeline waited.

"I once killed a man, Angie; fact is, I've killed two," Henry blurted out. "That bothers me considerable. then there's the Indians. I've killed more Indians than I can count and I've killed them about every way it can be done. I've seen the men in L Troop die, some quick, some slow and some not quite. But I guess the thing that's really bulgin' my craw is that day on the Little Big Horn. I've seen more death than any man rightly oughtta see. When you hear the death scream of men too many times, it sticks in your ears and you keep on hearin' it. I guess the glory I came lookin' for out here got splattered up with the blood of the men standin' next to me."

The rumbling of the wagon and the rhythmic beat of the horses' hoofs had a mesmerizing effect on Henry and his thoughts drifted back over the long trail he had come. He thought about his mother and sisters and wondered if they were still on the farm. He remembered the wonderful food and the conversation, and the kindness of the Weatherbee family on the banks of the Mississippi. He had left his home ten years ago and so much had happened in that time. He recalled Jefferson City and the Wanted poster and his fight in Wichita with Mule Harris--he wondered if Scat had found another partner. He listened again to the echoing sound of Taps at Kit Carson's funeral during his first day at Fort Bent and his heart sped a little as he saw in his mind's eye Old Glory snapping in the breeze at countless reveilles. In spite of himself he relived some of the dreadful hours of the Battle of the Little Big Horn. All of this since he'd left home ten years ago.

In Ohio he had had a dream and followed it, but it had turned into a nightmare and a pile of ashes. Now he had a wife and a wagon, but no dream, yet he felt the beginning of a strange new peace. It dawned on him then that this was what he had started out to search for so long ago.

Henry glanced at his wife's face against his shoulder and wondered if she had fallen asleep. At that moment, she opened her eyes and smiled at him and Henry felt his love for her surge up within him. "Missus Powell, I reckon you're a right smart female," he said. "We've been on this trip not more than an hour and already I can begin to see the sense in it. If'n it's all the same to you, I'd be pleased to let the discussion of my past lay awhile afore I give you a recitation. Fact is, I'd kinda like to leave it all back at Fort Bent."

"If that 's what you want to do, Henry, it's all right with me," Angeline said as she kissed him.

Henry's smile reached all the way to his toes. "All the talkin' from now one will be about our future. By the way," he added, "there's somethin I did leave at Fort Bent."

"Oh? What might that be?"

"The whiskey." Henry felt the sudden squeeze on his arm, a sign of his wife's pleasure at the news, and he was more proud of himself than at any time he could remember. He looked out past the canvas covering of the wagon. "There's a sunrise behind us that looks like the glory on the morning of creation," he said, almost reverently.

They made their first camp by a stream of swiftly-moving water. The grass was tall around the clearing and Henry tramped it down to build their fire. After they ate and while the horses grazed and drank, Henry and Angeline talked. The wall of waving grass was a haven from all they had left behind and they talked and planned and loved as if they had a new world to build. They talked of finding a valley somewhere in the west where the grass was thick and green, with a spring of clear water; a cabin that Henry would build with a big fireplace and lots of windows; a garden for Angeline and acres of land where Henry would raise cattle. They talked of children and chickens, of berry patches and cottonwood trees, of roses and radishes and newborn lambs, and the love in their hearts blended together. Only the sun and a red-winged blackbird saw how long their lips were pressed together and how long they stayed in each other's arms.

When they finally made ready to leave, Henry had a brand-new dream in his heart; a heart already filled to the top with happiness. It would have burst if Angeline had chosen that particular moment to tell him that he was to be a father. But with the timidity of the women of that era, she decided to wait until tomorrow and by doing so, it turned out that Henry never knew.

CHAPTER TWELVE
The Road to Buell

Yellow Wolf was the second son of Chief Last Bull and a full brother to Spotted Beaver. If anything happened to Spotted Beaver, Yellow Wolf would be chief of the Northern Cheyenne. But that all changed the night Colonel MacHenry attacked Dull Knife's camp on the Powder River.

Last Bull sent Dull Knife with the women and children to the camp of Crazy Horse on the Upper Big Horn for their safety. The bulk of the braves under Spotted Beaver were to engage the attacking pony soldiers in a rear guard action.

To Yellow Wolf and a small band of warriors Last Bull assigned the honor of preserving and protecting the tribe's highly-valued bundle of holy arrows. Proud of the task assigned to him, Yellow Wolf rode through the confusion of the camp to the teepee of Red Haw, the medicine man, and grabbed up the bundle of arrows, tying them to his own body. In his frantic haste to get the arrows to safety, he leaped his pony over a huge campfire and headed toward the spot where the group of Cheyenne who were to guard him on his ride through the night would be waiting. He rode to the edge of the camp, but no warriors waited there.

He spun his horse in circles and hunted in all directions until he had no more time to search for them and finally decided to ride alone. Bending low over his pony's neck, he raced into the blackness beyond the camp, riding headlong into a group of cavalrymen on a flanking maneuver; he now knew why his guards had fled.

His horse was shot in half a dozen places and when it crashed to the ground he knew no more. When consciousness returned, the sound of the night wind in the trees and the sight of a cold moon told him he was still alive, but the bundle of arrows was gone and Yellow Wolf was in disgrace.

The next evening he sat in the teepee of Crazy Horse and told his story to Dull Knife and his father, Last

Bull. When he finished, he waited in silence for the judgment of the three mighty chiefs.

A piece of beaver skin and a strip from the pelt of a wolf were attached to the buffalo robe that covered his father's shoulders. Last Bull wore them as symbols of his pride in his two sons. Now, with deliberation, he tore the wolf pelt off and dropped it in the fire before him. As the smoke from burning fur rose around him, he delivered his judgment. "From this day on I have only one son, Spotted Beaver. My second son is dead and as long as my days shall be counted, no Cheyenne will be known as Yellow Wolf." Raising his eyes to his son, he continued. "You without a name cannot be Cheyenne, so you must leave the camp of Crazy Horse and appear no more before my eyes. Take with you those who ran from the pony soldiers on the Powder River and leave the land of the Cheyenne forever."

Yellow Wolf and his band of fifteen braves rode southwest. They crossed the North Platte and continued up the full length of the Tongue River Valley. They were bitter and angry over what they considered the injustice of their fate. They were now outcasts and in their savage breasts burned a craving to kill, to wreak vengeance on anything that lived.

On the evening of the third day after they left the camp of Crazy Horse, they rode to the top of a rise and sat surveying the grasslands beyond. Yellow Wolf moved apart from the others and chose the highest spot to gaze from. The rays of the late afternoon sun glistened on the darkly tanned skin of his naked arms and chest as he sat motionless, only the feathers in his scalp lock moving in the gentle breeze. His black eyes peered out from a hideous mask of warpaint, searching for any signs of life.

The sun dropped lower and still they sat. Finally, Yellow Wolf's keen eyes spotted a thin thread of smoke rising from a faroff clump of trees. Lame Dog and Little Horse had also seen the smoke. They grunted their discovery, but Yellow Wolf had already turned his pony and was riding off the ridge.

****

I'll tell him tonight, Angeline thought, after he's filled his stomach. It's always best to tell a man he's going to be a father when you've just fed him a good meal. Angeline was at the tailgate of the wagon, mixing the spoon bread she would make in the big black skillet now heating over the fire. She was humming as she stirred and feeling happier than she ever had. She glanced lovingly at her husband's back as he headed to the river.

She was reaching for another cup of cornmeal when Yellow Wolf grabbed her. She could not understand what was happening until he spun her around and she looked with horror at his painted face. Then, Yellow Wolf released her and touched the long, black hair that fell over her shoulders. Angeline screamed and he struck her across the mouth with a powerful blow. She fell across the wagon gate and slid to the ground.

Henry heard her scream and ran for the camp. When he broke into the clearing Lame Dog and Little Horse each grabbed an arm. Without breaking stride he flipped them from him and they spun to the ground. He crashed into Yellow Wolf and clutched the intruder's throat in a death grip. The other Indians rose from the tall grass and one of them clubbed Henry across the back of the head with his rifle butt. Henry's grip relaxed and he fell into blackness.

When he came to, he was seated on the ground, his arms bound to the wagon wheel with strips of rawhide. The sight that met his eyes tore into his brain like the blade of a knife. Angeline lay on the ground not ten feet away, completely naked, a rope of rawhide stretched across her stomach and staked to the ground. Her arms were outstretched and an Indian stood on each hand. Another stood on her hair, which had been spread out behind her. As Henry watched, one Indian rose from between her legs and another stood in line waiting his turn. The savages were laughing and those who had already taken their pleasure with Angeline were ramsacking the wagon. None of them paid any attention to Henry, although he strained at his bonds and screamed his fury at them. Angeline's moans and cries were tipping his sanity.
Finally, the last of the men took his turn, then walked

away to claim his share of the loot. Left alone, Angeline rolled her head to look at her husband. "We were..." Henry heard her say. Then her eyes closed and she lay motionless. Henry strained at the thongs with all the power of his mighty body as the demand for revenge churned his insides like a tornado. Pulling his feet up into a squatting position, he began to rock the wagon.

Yellow Wolf chose that moment to mount his warriors, but first he strode to Henry and placed the tip of his scalping knife against Henry's throat. The point brought blood, then he backed off, and with his black eyes flaming with hatred, he said, "Buffalo Walks Like A Man now watch squaw die!"

He walked over to Angeline and twisted his left hand in her long black hair. He lifted her head, and with one sweep of his knife, the top of her head was gone. Henry screamed and threw himself in desperation against his bonds. Yellow Wolf looked back at the bound man, then, in an act of defiance he swung his knife in a sweeping slash that opened Angeline's stomach.

Yellow Wolf trotted to his pony and mounted. As he rode by the campfire, he grasped a stick out of the fire that still glowed at one end, whirled it above his head until it burst into flame, then tossed it into the wagon behind Henry. Wheeling his horse, he and his band of renegades were swallowed up in the tall grass.

Henry's struggle to free himself was done in a raging fury. As his great muscles expanded against his bonds, the rawhide cut into his flesh and blood ran down his arms. He threw his head from side to side as he lunged again and again against the straps that held him. His eyes were those of a maddened animal and spittle dripped from his chin.

As the flames in the wagon leaped higher, exhaustion overtook him and he slumped forward. The fire ran along the center of the canvas cover, which burned through and slid toward the ground. A corner of the flaming cloth dropped across the rawhide binding Henry's hands behind his back and ate through it, strand after strand, until he was freed and fell forward.

The sun went down like the wick of a lamp until it

was out and there was darkness on the land. The wagon burned slowly, the light from the flames playing across the still bodies of Henry and Angeline Powell. Henry's mind had hidden under a blanket of horror, much as he himself had hidden from unknown terrors of the night as a boy. The small flames in the wagon bed skipped into the air and were gone and the embers dropped to the ground. Still, nothing moved except the darkness as it closed in. The moon rose and had cleared the top of the trees when Henry finally lifted his head.

He sat on the ground with his hands covering his face while the moon moved another foot across the sky. Then he got to his feet and went to search for something that he could use to dig a grave. He remembered the wooden bucket he had dropped at the edge of the trees when he had heard Angeline scream, so he retrieved it and broke out one of the staves, using it to dig a grave for his wife in the soft, loamy ground. He did not hurry, but dug it deep and wide. He filled the grave with buffalo grass.

When he was finished, he pulled Angeline's body into the soft, green bed and covered her with more arm-loads of grass. Then he filled the grave, building a mound of the black soil. When he finished, he turned away, compassionless and unemotional. The venom of hatred filled his being so full there was no room for love or sentiment or sorrow.

In a way, Henry Powell died that afternoon along with Angeline. The thing that survived and lived on was only a shell, filled with fierce bitterness and only one emotion; revenge, quick and total, was to nurture his soul and body from that day on. Never again would he see beauty or feel compassion or reason with sanity. A pile of ashes and a spot of bloodsoaked ground marked the end of the second and last of Henry Powell's dreams. Without a thought or a backward look, he crossed the river and started his search for Yellow Wolf. From now on, every Indian would be Yellow Wolf in his tormented mind.

Long after Henry departed, the black skillet on the circle of stones slipped and fell to the ground, frightening a chipmunk that had been feeding on Angeline's spilled cornmeal. He perched on top of the mound of black earth for a moment, them disappeared into the tall grass leaving only silence.

According to Sgt. Dan O'Malley, Henry showed up at Fort Ruby, Nevada Territory, walked straight to the blacksmith's shop and, without a word to anyone, picked up a hammer and set to work. His broad shoulders and massive arms were burned brown, his hair was long and a beard hid most of his face. His shoes were worn out and his trousers were in tatters. Just who he was or where he had come from, no one knew. He established himself with such finality and defiance that it never occurred to anyone to question his motives or tell him to leave.

However, the long hours he spent at the forge and the quality and quantity of his work soon convinced the company farrier that he was a good man to have around. He was never officially hired; Sgt. O'Malley simply shared a small portion of his pay with the strange giant who swung an eight-pound hammer tirelessly from sunup to sundown.

On the evening of the first day of the month, he would leave a few coins on Henry's anvil. The next morning, Henry would carry them to the sutler's and put them on credit toward whiskey and chewing tobacco until the first of the next month. The Sergeant was soon able to calculate the amount of money necessary to keep Henry in whiskey and tobacco for a month, and that became the precise amount of Henry's pay. He gave Henry a pair of shoes and pants and a faded Army blouse.

The months rolled by. The fort's commander was replaced, then replaced again, the second replacement being Capt. Keogh, now a Colonel. One day as he walked across the parade ground, he passed close to the blacksmith's shop and the figure of Henry Powell caught his eye. He stopped and studied the man, tugged by some long-ago memory, but when Henry raised his head and the Colonel saw his eyes, he walked on with a shake of his head.

Then, toward evening of a cold January day, Sgt. O'Malley's attention was drawn to the abrupt cessation of the rhythmic pounding of Henry's hammer. Something had attracted Henry's attention out front. The Sergeant looked and saw a mounted patrol escorting a half naked Indian on a spotted pony toward headquarters. As they passed the shop, Henry suddenly bellowed, "YELLOW WOLF!" and drew back the eight-pound hammer to hurl it with the velocity of a cannonball straight at the Indian. It struck the savage just above the ear and his head exploded like a pumpkin. Henry grabbed an iron bar with a glowing tip from the forge and was upon the indian almost before he hit the ground. Before any of the soldiers could react, Henry raised the smoking iron high into the air and drove it through the Indian's chest.

Later, in the guardhouse, Sgt. O'Malley talked to Henry through the barred door. "What in red eyed snakes got into you? Who's this Yellow Wolf you were hollerin' about? That was Iron Shirt you brained."

"It was Yellow Wolf," Henry declared.

"That was Iron Shirt," the Sergeant insisted, "the son of a Shoshone chief who rode in from camp on the Snake River to powwow with the Colonel. When Iron Shirt's father learns about this, he'll raise hell and put a prop under it. Come tomorrow, the Old Man is goin' to chop you up and fry the pieces."

The Sergeant's prediction never came true because the next morning Henry was gone. He had been shackled hand and foot and chained to the wall, but the chain had been pulled free and the bars ripped from the rear window like straws from a broom. Also missing was a canvas bag of blacksmithing tools, evidently taken to cut his shackles.

Mounted patrols were sent in all directions and they searched for three days, but Henry left hardly any trail at all. He had learned the Indian trick of backtracking in a stream, coming out on a rock, leaping a great distance and reentering the stream, then backtracking again. He had acquired the Indian cleverness of covering his trail and while his followers spent endless time unraveling his tracks, he put miles between himself and them by running tirelessly hour after hour.

Henry traveled for three days and crossed over into the Ponderosa pine country in northern Arizona Territory. He gave no thought to where he was going and cared less. He was very hungry and tired and when he came upon a small lake, he decided to take care of both problems. He cut a sapling, sharpened one end and notched a barb near the point, them waded into the water. In a short time, he speared a trout. With flint and steel he soon had a fire going and quickly roasted and devoured his catch. Then he stretched out in the warm sun and slept. He repeated the performance the next morning for breakfast before heading south. When he dropped down into the desert country, his diet changed from fish to rabbit.

At first his mind was occupied with relishing the moment of revenge when he had killed the Indian he believed to be Yellow Wolf. Then, after a night or two in the soothing silence of the desert, thoughts of the futility of his situation tugged at his mind. He had no regrets or remorse, no emotions of any kind as a matter of fact; all that was buried under a mound of earth, hundreds of miles behind him. The instinctive desire, weak as it was, to find food and shelter and seek others of his kind moved him merely because it was his only feeling. In that way, the trail of Henry Powell cut the road to Buell.

Henry stood in the middle of the road and looked ahead to where it disappeared into the mouth of a canyon. the heat of the sun was great, but above the mountains that formed the canyon he saw a black cloud, moving rapidly. The thought of coolness in the shadow of the cloud started him walking up the road to Buell. He could just as easily have walked in the opposite direction.

He passed the mouth of the canyon and reached the edge of the town when the storm broke with a sound like a hundred cannons. The downpour seemed protective and comforting, and in some strange way, Henry felt akin to the fury and thunder of the storm. It was like a friend who understood how things were and for a moment his spirits brightened. He strode with purpose and anticipation to the front door of the China Girl Saloon. A thunderous clap from the storm followed him inside. Henry Powell had arrived in Buell.

CHAPTER THIRTEEN
Doc Jarka

Doc Jarka was a wiry little man with a dark complexion, a heavy mustache and a bald head. His movements were quick, his wit was sharp and he smelled eternally of medicines. He always wore a vest under his suit coat, its pockets bulging with tongue depressors, pill bottles, black cigars, a pen or two and a thermometer. He was a good doctor, knowledgeable, blessed with a instinct for diagnosis and amply endowed with the courage of his convictions.

His father, who had been a doctor in Poland, moved his family to Boston in 1859. Doc was then fifteen years old and two years later he started his premedical studies as one of the youngest students ever to enter Harcourt University. He finished his internship when he was twenty-five and entered private practice, soon to be one of the most sought-after doctors in Boston, the darling of the social set. His wealthy clientele grew in numbers as the years went by and his bank account increased correspondingly.

By the time he was thirty, his sixteen-hour days had become a physical and mental burden and he began to seek support from a frequent glass of bourbon. He had a maid, a houseboy, a Chinese cook and a luxurious apartment overlooking the river. He liked the bachelor life and since he had no time for courting anyway, he accepted his destiny to remain a bachelor. He was on the staff of four city hospitals and it was prophesied that he would one day be Chief of Staff at Massachussetts General.

He performed feats of surgery that were the talk of the medical world. He pushed himself to do more and more, often performing three and four operations a day, frequently spending twelve hours bent over a table with only a few minutes between patients. His stamina seemed inexhaustible and only one or two of his closest colleagues knew of the large quantities of liquor he was consuming to keep going.

Older heads knew that he would not be able to keep up the pace long and they pleaded with him to take some time off, to go to the North Woods to fish and hunt and rest. He always agreed it was a good idea and he would do it next month, but there was always so much to do and so many patients waiting that next month was always booked solid.

Eventually, he reached the point where he started the day by drinking a large glass filled with a little orange juice and a lot of bourbon. He then shaved and bathed, ate breakfast and arrived at the hospital a little before seven. The months rolled by and even those critical of how he was pushing himself were almost ready to admit that maybe the man was indestructible.

But Doc knew differently. He began to feel the increasing weight of his fatigue. His heretofore stone-steady hands began to tremble and he found he had an obsession to do more and more. His answer to his problems was to increase his intake of liquor.

The end of his career as a Boston surgeon came about in a manner puzzling and terrifying to him. He left home at his usual time and rode in a hansom cab through the nearly empty streets of Boston. It was snowing hard and he had scheduled abdominal surgery for seven o'clock, leaving instructions to have the patient ready at that hour. He knew that a challenging and delicate piece of work awaited him and he was anxious to get at it.

His patient was Mrs. Turner, the wife of a doctor on the staff. When he reached the prep room, Dr. Osborn, who was to assist him, was already scrubbing. Within thirty minutes, he, too, was scrubbed and gowned and ready. He entered the operating room with his usual briskness, took the chart from the nurse and studied it, then stepped to the side of his patient.

Her abdomen lay bare, the assisting nurse was at his right elbow and Dr. Osborn stepped to his left side. The mark for the incision had been drawn and he extended his right hand for the scalpel. It slammed into his palm with a familiar impact. And at that instant, he began to fall apart. He suddenly became weak, sweat broke out on his face, and his hands shook violently. He could not remember where he was. The scalpel fell to the floor and he sank to his knees. Dr. Osborn took over the operation while he was helped to a bed in a nearby room.

The news spread quickly throughout the hospital. His condition was diagnosed as a nervous breakdown caused by extreme mental and physical fatigue. He was wheeled to a private room and treatment was begun immediately. It would be a long road to complete recovery.

As fate would have it, Dr. Turner was assigned to Doc's case. He was aware of the situation and planned a course for extensive treatment.
Throughout his stay in Room 107, the flow of flowers and plants from Doc's many patients never ceased. The high esteem in which he was held by the entire hospital staff afforded him constant care and attention. For days, his progress was negligible and when it started it was slow and the days began to run into weeks.
At last, however, the day arrived when Dr. Turner agreed that he could travel to a small resort in Maine for further rest and therapy. The morning he was to leave, he was wheeled past the nurses' station and he stopped to say goodbye. "By the way, how is Mrs. Turner doing?" he asked the head nurse.

She paused for a long moment then replied, "Mrs. Turner died on the operating table."

He did not make the trip to the resort in Maine. Instead, he went home, arranged for the maid to pack a trunk and a couple of bags, paid off his help and drove to the train depot. He bought a one-way ticket to Salt Lake City and left Boston, never to return.

Doc detrained in Salt Lake City on a beautiful spring day in mid-April of 1875. He was immediately fascinated with the sprawling city. Most of the buildings were one story, unlike the avenues of tall buildings in his native Boston, and he was mildly intoxicated with the clean, crisp air he breathed. Already, he felt better than he had in years. He liked the freedom from the concrete canyons of the big city and the thought that there was no appointment awaiting him, today, tomorrow, or ever if he wanted it that way.

He set off up the street with all the eagerness and abandonment of a colt turned out to pasture, walking for some distance and taking in the sights and sounds of the western town. The sounds were friendly and the people smiled and nodded.

He spotted a barber pole and decided to treat himself to a shave. It had been a long while since he could afford the time for the hot-toweled luxury of a barbershop shave. He stretched out in the chair and closed his eyes and the barber went to work doing wonderful things with the towels, lather, a keen razor and witch hazel.

In due time, Doc found living quarters on the second floor of a large old home on Taber Street. It was a white adobe building with an outside stairway leading up to the three rooms he had rented. The branches of an elm tree growing on the north side of the house overhung the low wall that enclosed the roof and Doc spent most of his days up there. He watched the sun rise over distant mountains while sitting in a rocking chair with his feet propped on the wall, and when the sun was overhead, he moved to the shade of the elm. He could almost feel the strength returning to his body and the peace to his mind. The sounds of the hospital were swept away be the music of songbirds and the smell of anesthetic was smothered by the fragrance of jasmine.

When he began taking strolls along the streets, something always occurred that sent him home feeling a significant event had taken place. One afternoon, he came upon a lady who was stranded on the limb of an apple tree. She had a pail in her hand and had been harvesting the apples, but to reach the best ones higher up, she had stepped from the top of the ladder onto a limb and had knocked it over. He righted the ladder, then turned his head while the lady descended, blushing as she thanked him for his assistance. She offered him an apple as a reward.

"That's a beauty!" he said. "What kind is it?"

"A Maidenblush," she answered.

"My favorite." He saw a boy in a meadow trying unsuccessfully to keep a kite in the air. He watched the boy run with the kite until the wind caught it, then watched as it dipped and darted and finally banged to the ground. He diagnosed the trouble and walked over to the boy. "You need more weight on the tail, son." He took a kerchief out of his pocket, knotted a small stone in one end and tied the other end to the tail of the kite. "Now put 'er up," he said.

The boy took the kite to the other end of the field and began to run back with it. By the time he reached Doc the kite was riding the wind as steadily as a schooner.

"Gee thanks, Mister," the boy said and he beamed. He watched the kite grow smaller and smaller in the evening sky and felt as if he had just performed one of the major accomplishments of his life. Finally, patting his young friend on the head, he headed home whistling.

The really big day, however, came the afternoon he met Mr. McIntyre. Each morning at sunrise he had noticed a steeple in the distance and decided, this morning, to visit the church. It was a long walk and on the way back he stopped under the shade of a tree to rest. He had just taken out one of his thin black cigars, bit off the end, and was applying fire to it when someone said, "You a checker player?"

He looked up and saw an older gentleman in a rocking chair on the porch of a small house close by. His hair and beard were gray and steel-rimmed glasses sat low on his nose.

"What was that?" he asked.

"I asked if you're a checker player?" the old man repeated.

"Well now, it just happens that I've never been beaten by anybody east of the Mississippi," he answered.

"Peculiar," said the old man. "I've never been beaten by anyone west of it!"

"You challenging?" he asked.

"You accepting?" the old man responded.

"I don't see as how I have an alternative."

"There's a 'tater crate over there. Bring it over and sit down. By the way, my name's Herman McIntyre. Folks hereabouts call me Josh."

"I'm Doc Jarka, Josh. Pleased to meet you."

"Same here," said Josh.

The old man picked up a block of wood which was lying by his chair and put it between them. He aroused the hound dog that had been sleeping on the checkerboard and, unfolding it, laid it on the block. He reached into one shirt pocket and took out a handful of white checkers which he handed to Doc, then from the other pocket he drew out the black ones. Soon, the pieces were all arranged on the board and the game began. There was no conversation.

Josh was a good player, there was no doubt about that. Twice he thought he had tricked Doc into making the wrong move and his eyes snapped with glee, but both times Doc avoided the trap and the old man's disappointment showed. But he concentrated all the more and very slowly and cleverly set a trap. When Doc placed his hand on the crucial checker to make his move, the old man held his breath in anticipation. If Doc took the bait and moved the checker to the left, all Josh's cleverness would be for nothing. But if he moved it to the right, the game would be over and Josh would be the winner.

Slowly, Doc started moving the checker to the left, watching the old man grow tense out of the corners of his eyes, then he pulled it back, hesitated, a moment, and moved it to the right, lifting his hand.

"I've got you," the old man hollered joyfully as he cleaned the board of Doc's checkers.

"Well," Doc said, "at least I'm still champion back East," and he stood to leave.

"Afore you go," said Josh, "wet your whistle." He hauled out a jug from under the rocker. "Made this cider myself," he said as he poured a tin cup full for Doc. "It'll take the kinks out of a pig's tail!"

He played checkers with Josh three times a week from them on and never once did he win. Often it would appear that he had the old man beaten, but he would always manage to make one wrong move and Josh would always shout with glee. They never talked about their families or their pasts.

Then, one day in September, he came by for their game and Josh's rocker was empty. The checkerboard and the cider jug were there, but the hound and the old man were gone. He went home and returned the following day and the next, but still no Josh. He decided against going to the door or talking to the neighbors because, whatever had happened, he did not want to know.

The city of Salt Lake lost a little of its sparkle after that. He began to grow restless and finally realized he was developing an urge to move on. One morning, when he walked uptown to replenish his supply of cigars, he passed a poolroom and noticed the large blackboard on the front of the building. He stopped and read:

> MEN WANTED
> For Wagon train to Goldfields of Arizona
>
> | Drivers | 12 |
> | --- | --- |
> | Cooks | 2 |
> | Cook's helper | 1 |
> | Blacksmiths | 2 |
> | Harness maker | 1 |
> | Carpenters | 2 |
> | Butcher | 1 |
> | Doctor | 1 |
> | Outriders | 4 |
> | Guides | 2 |

Departure May 1, Lord willing and the creek don't rise. All wanting to sign on see Benjamin Merriweather, Wagon master office, Ace Poolroom.

He knew he was going to sign on, even while he was arguing the pros and cons with himself. He suddenly felt young again.

Ben Merriweather was a big hulk of a man and endowed with a natural air of authority so that when he spoke, people obeyed. He was a good wagonmaster and had traveled nearly every trail through the west a number of times. He invited Doc to share his wagon and by the time they were three days on the trail the two men had achieved a mutual trust and understanding.

"Just how much doctoring you had?" Ben asked one evening.

"Enough to get by," Doc answered. "I can lance a boil or stop a nosebleed."

Everything went well for the first ten days, but when they entered the desert country of the Navajos, one of the wagons became bogged down in the sand. Poles, flattened on one end to be used as pinch bars, were put under each wheel with two men on each pole, and at a signal from the teamster they threw their weight against them.

During the operation, a pole under one of the front wheels slipped and struck the twelve-year old son of Bill and Mary Harvey, knocking him sprawling. At the same time, the driver started the teams and before anyone could move, the steel-rimmed wheel of the heavy supply wagon passed over the boy's left leg just above the knee. Ben lifted young Ned in his arms and headed for the lead wagon, calling for Doc as he went.

Doc was having coffee with the teamsters but he knew by the tone of Ben's voice that there had been trouble. He had been in enough emergencies in his life to know the value of preparedness, so by the time Ben arrived carrying the boy, he had his medical bag open and was waiting.

Ben explained what had happened and Doc went quickly to work, issuing orders to these rugged men of the trail with the same coolness and authority as he had used with trained nurses in numerous operating rooms. "Unlash two barrels from the wagons and get some planking. Set me up a table, and MOVE! Some of you put a kettle of water on the fire. I'll need some help. Mrs Christenson, you'll be my assistant."

Mary Harvey was hovering over her son, trying to comfort him as he cried out in pain. Bill Harvey asked, "What can I do to help?"

"Gather up about four belts and bring a skinning knife," Doc answered.

The makeshift table was set up in the shade of the wagon. Ben laid the boy gently on the table and made a pillow of his hat for the youngster's head. His father returned with the belts.

"Thread these belts through the planks and buckle

them tightly over his chest, stomach and thighs. Bill, you hold Ned's other leg down tight." He slit the trouser on the injured leg clear to the waist with the skinning knife, them gently explored the damage with his talented fingers. The group stood in silence, watching, as he carefully turned the knee from side to side. All this took only a few seconds and while he was digging into his bag for drugs to relieve Ned's pain, his mind was diagnosing the problem and the possible treatments. Ned responded quickly to the sedative and began to quiet down.

"How bad is it, Doc?" Ben asked.

"There's one break in the bone above the knee and possibly more, I can't be sure. But the real damage is to the muscles. The ligaments are torn loose from the knee, the tissues are badly damaged, and there's massive internal hemorrhaging. There'll be extensive swelling; in fact, it's already started.

"Now Ben, here's what I want you to do. I noticed this morning that there's still snow on the slopes of that mountain ahead of us. Can't be more than seven or eight miles, so pick your two best riders, put them on the fastest mounts you've got and tell them to run the legs off the horses if necessary. Have them each take a piece of canvas and bring back all the snow they can carry; it'll hold down the swelling."

Ben was off at a run and Doc switched his attention to Mrs. Christenson. "Cut the pant leg off, bathe the leg with cold water and then bathe it a second time." He turned to the group who were waiting to help if they could. "I'll need several yards of bandage, so tear up sheets or skirts or anything that'll do. I'll also need two splints about three feet long and a bucket of tar."

The boy's father stood holding his son's leg against the table. "He's going to be all right, through, isn't he, Doc?" he asked.

"Right now I'm going to set the bones before the swelling gets too bad, and after that we'll just have to see. You must understand that the boy's leg was crushed and the vessels and arteries were torn and ruptured. The circulation has been stopped so the leg will swell to twice its size and turn black. The swelling tends to restrict the circulation even more, so our job is to get it to go down as quickly as possible. That's why I've sent for the snow. We'll make packs for the boy's leg and if that doesn't work, then we'll have a problem," he concluded.

"What problem?"

"Gangrene."

"Supposin' gangrene comes; you can treat that, can't you?"

"No, Bill, there is no treatment. I'd have to take the boy's leg off."

"Oh, dear God!" Bill groaned.

"Don't go borrowing trouble," he said. "You go look after your wife."

Mrs. Christenson pulled on the leg as he instructed and he felt the bone snap into place. The problem now was to splint it without binding the swollen areas. The best he could do was to put one splint under the leg and another on top, extending just over the kneecap so the boy's movements would disturb the broken bone as little as possible. The leg was first wrapped in clean white bandages, then bound tightly in strips dipped in tar. Layer after layer was applies until the leg was encased in a tube of black pitch that would stiffen and hold the leg and splints rigid.

In considerably less than two hours the riders were back with the snow. Doc had already ordered a hole dug in the cool earth and lined with canvas. After he filled a wooden bucket for immediate use, the remaining snow was dumped into the hole and the canvas folded over it.

Evening came upon them, so lanterns were lit and the long vigil began. Ned's leg was kept packed in snow, but as the night wore on Doc felt more than a little concern. To complicate matters, the boy developed a fever and toward morning he became delirious. His father came by half a dozen times during the night to stand at the boy's side a while, them walk away.

Daylight revealed a badly swollen leg. Doc packed it in snow again and sat down to think while he ate breakfast. He never left the boy throughout the day. Ned's fever raged and he tossed in delirium. Frequently, as he was packing the leg, he would rub some of the snow on the boy's forehead and neck. He refused lunch and supper, but by the time darkness fell he could see no improvement; if anything, the situation had worsened.

Again the lanterns were lit and another blanket was placed across Ned's feverish body. Doc was frustrated because, with all his medical knowledge, there was so little he could do. Each time he took the boy's temperature it was up a half degree and his concern mounted.

During the night, people came by to see if they could help, but to each Doc only shook his head. Ben finally asked the question that everyone else was thinking. "Is the boy going to be all right, Doc?"

Doc looked at him through weary eyes. "You're double-damned right he is!" he said and returned to his work.

Hours later, he walked to the campfire to toss on some wood and pour himself another cup of coffee. How many hours had it been? He returned to find Ned sleeping peacefully and when he put his hand to the boy's forehead, he realized the fever had broken. Relieved, he tucked the blanket around Ned's shoulders, them, looking toward the pinkness coming over the eastern horizon, he said to no one in particular, "By golly, it's going to be a fine day." He reached for one of his cigars and made a ceremony of lighting it. He twirled it in his mouth and shoved his hands into his coat pockets. Looking over at his now recovering patient between rich puffs of smoke, he said "Yes sir, it's going to be a really fine day!"

He saw Ben approaching and answered the question he knew was coming. "The boy is fine," he said. "I want some of your men to rig up a hammock and swing it from the hoops inside our wagon. Soon as Ned and I get some sleep we can pull out of here." Without waiting for an answer he headed for the wagon, trailing cigar smoke as he went.

Ben decided they could afford to spend one more day and night in camp and that was how long Doc and Ned slept. The morning they were to pull out Bill Harvey came by to pay Doc, but he would have none of it. "It's my job to take care of the sick; that's what I hired on for.

I'll settle for a handshake and a beer when we hit Tucson," he told the grateful father.

They shook hands and Bill said, "You can have a dozen beers, Doc. Mary and I will always be beholden to you."

Doc spent much of his time that first day in the wagon with Ned. He was pleased to see that the swelling in the leg was going down and the color was returning to normal. During the day Ned asked, "Is my leg going to be all right, Doc? Will I be able to walk?"

"Walk? Why, son, you'll be able to outrun a jack-rabbit before the summer's half over."

"That night after the evening meal, Doc found a box with a note attached that said, "To Doc Jarka from Bill and Mary Harvey with many thanks and God's blessings." Inside, he found a number of items: a poke of sassafrass bark, a jar of blueberry jelly Mary had brought all the way from her native Wisconsin, another jar of spiced peaches, a package of maple sugar candy and a small pruned rosebush with the roots bound in muslin and labeled "Seven sisters". Doc looked at each item carefully and his heart warmed. The Harveys had shared with him what they treasured most; he decided it was the richest fee he had ever received. These are the kind of people I want to work among the rest of my days, he told himself.

He replaced the items in the box and still had them when he arrived in Buell three months later.

Ben led the wagon train through the Sutherland Valley and into Tucson in mid-June of 1878. It had been agreed that this was as far as Ben was to take them. From Tucson, each prospector was to light out toward the mountain range of his choice. Ben told Doc he expected to head another train bound for California and invited his friend to go along.

"No," Doc said. "I guess I've eaten enough trail dust for a while. I'll just stay here in Tucson for a time and see what turns up. Maybe the town needs a first-rate doctor."

They built their last campfire and ate their last meal together on the banks of the Santa Cruz River. Ben paid off his men, farewells were said, and most of the travelers turned in so they could get an early start the next morning on their chosen courses.

Doc borrowed a horse and rode into town. He wanted some information so he decided to look up the nearest bartender. He stopped at the Congress Saloon, found a spot at the busy bar, and ordered a mug of beer. Tables of poker were going strong and the air was heavy with the smell of kerosene and cigar smoke.

He had given up trying to get information from the busy bartender when a man wearing a star on his vest walked in. As the lawman approached, Doc said, "I'm a stranger in town. My name is Doc Jarka."

"Pleased to meet you," said the young man. "I'm Deputy Pruitt."

"Join me in a beer?" Doc asked, motioning to the bartender. "I want to buy a team and a buckboard. You wouldn't know anyone who had a rig for sale, would you?"

"I reckon I might just know who to send you to," said the deputy. "Fellow by the name of Rafe Ochoa deals in horses some."

"Good! Where can I find the gentleman?"

The deputy drained his mug, wiped his mouth on his sleeve and answered, "He's sittin' at that table yonder, the fella with his back to you, packin' those pearl-handled six guns. But before you talk to him, check his pile of chips; if he's winnin' I don't believe I'd bother him--he gets a mite touchy."

Doc got a refill on his beer and sidled over to the poker table. It appeared that Rafe was having a bad night and the man sitting opposite him was apparently the heavy winner. Rafe was a handsome man, with long sideburns and a closely trimmed mustache and he wore a ruby pin in his green ascot tie. As Doc watched, the man to his left was the only one bucking the heavy winner.

"I call," the man said as he pushed a stack of chips to the center of the table. "What you so proud of?"

"Three aces," was the answer.

"Hell's fire! You got too much luck for me," said the caller and threw his cards in.

The winner put his hand face up on the table and

reached for the pot. "Took a little luck," he said. "I drew the ace of hearts."

From the corner of his eye, Doc saw Rafe's left hand go to the collar at the back of his coat, then there was a flash of steel and a thud as a bone-handled dagger pinned the three aces to the tabletop. "It just happens, mister," he said, "that I discarded the ace of hearts when I threw my hand in before the draw. Now, just how do you reckon it showed up in your hand?"

At the thud of the knife on the tabletop, Deputy Pruitt moved in, gun in hand. Doc thought the situation exciting and when it was over he settled into the vacant seat at the poker table. Three flushes and two full houses later, he owned a team of sorrels and a buckboard. He also became addicted to the game of poker.

He took a room with a family on West Alameda Street. He was very proud of his team and rig and he drove about town every day. Sometimes he explored the desert beyond the town limits and ranged as far as the Pantano Wash to the east and the San Xavier Mission to the south. During the day he stopped at the Congress Saloon to have a beer or two with Deputy Pruitt or to sit in for a while on one of the never-ending poker games.

He thought seriously about finding office space and hanging out his shingle, but although he liked Tucson, he wasn't ready. Then it dawned on him that the trouble was the people; there were too many of them and he wanted to live with people like his friends on the wagon train.

One day he visited Fort Lowell a few miles east of Tucson and his problem was solved. He had gone there to ask about the Territory and the neighboring towns and in the course of his chat with Maj. Dunkirk, the Major told him, "I know of a thriving little town in need of a doctor. It's a mining town in the Dragoon Mountains southeast of here, some eighty-ninety miles."

"I'll take a run over there. What's the name of the place?" Doc had asked.

"Buell," the Major replied.

CHAPTER FOURTEEN
The Death of Will Storms

The townsfolk never quite forgot Doc Jarka's arrival in Buell. Driving two bays hitched to a buckboard, he hit the main street one quiet afternoon like a small tornado. His team's ears were laid back as they rounded the turn coming into town, their nostrils flaring, and Doc was nipping them with the whip at every leap. When he cleared the turn he saw that he would soon run out of street, so he stood up and leaned back on the reins, seesawing the horses to a halt in a huge cloud of dust just short of the bridge.

Tucson had gotten too big for him and he often found himself taking a "thirty-minute ride," he said, "To hear a little silence." Having been told that Buell was in need of a doctor and thinking it might be a good place to hang out his shingle, he decided to drive over and look around.

He had stepped down and was tying his quivering team to the hitching rail in front of the general store when Frank Applegate came out to investigate the commotion.

"I'm Doc Jarka. I stopped by to see if you might be needing a doctor in this town."

"'Pears more like you flew in rather than stopped by," said Frank.

"Just an example of the service I give," Doc said with a sly grin. "What really happened was, the horses spooked and I was letting them run it out."

"Come on in," Frank invited. "Likely my wife has a pot of coffee on the stove."

"That's right kindly of you," Doc said. "I accept." He patted the rump of the trembling horse closest to him and followed Frank into the store. Frank led him to the living quarters in the back of the store.

"Opal, meet a newcomer to town. He's a doctor and thinkin' of settling here."

Opal was busy at the sink and only nodded her head in response to the introduction. Doc thought he had never seen such sadness on the face of a woman. Her large eyes were lifeless and misty and her movements indicated she had no interest in what she was doing. Frank brought two cups from the cupboard and motioned Doc into a chair by the table, then poured coffee from the granite pot on the stove. Respecting the unwritten law forbidding inquiry into a man's past, Frank opened the conversation by asking, "Travel far?"

"I came in from Tucson," Doc replied. "Didn't much care for it, though, too big. Thought I'd like a smaller place and I heard about Buell. Mining town, isn't it?"

Frank gulped a swallow of the black brew and rose. "Come here a minute." He led Doc to the side porch and pointed up the canyon. Doc saw the gaping hole of the mine and the tracks a thousand yards from where he stood. "That's the old Jefferson Buell mine," he said. One of the wagons was being loaded at the tipple and a couple of teamsters were hitching up a fresh team. "That fellow on the Appaloosa," Frank pointed, "is Tom Pender. He works for the White and Beasley Mining Company and has charge of the teams that haul the ore. We're mining silver here now. The gold old Jeff found wasn't deep but then they uncovered a vein of silver and that's when White and Beasley moved in. Word is, it's a pretty good vein. Nothin' like Tombstone, but they haul a right smart amount of ore out of here."

Doc listened intently as he watched the emptied ore car being pulled back up the track by a cable that ran through a pulley at the top of the hill and back down to a huge winch being turned by a team of mules. They went back in to finish their coffee. "Tell me a little about the town," he said.

Frank stared into his coffee for a while before answering. "To tell you the truth, it's a helluva place. It really isn't a town at all, just a collection of buildings. Folks don't do no neighboring'; there's no law and no church. There wouldn't be any schoolin' for the youngsters if it wasn't for Maude Ballinger. She runs the post office at the front of my store and I let her use the storeroom as a school in the afternoons. I don't know what keeps the damn town goin'.

"In the first place, it's laid out all wrong. The miners and their families all live down the canyon behind that pile of boulders you saw when you came in. That means main street gets used by the ore wagons and during rains it's a helluva mess." Frank paused in his story to refill their cups.

Doc lit a cigar. "Don't exactly sound like Happy Valley."

"A few of us been thinking of doing something about it," Frank continued. "Fact is we're gettin' together Saturday night here in the store to see what can be done. Might be you'd like to attend."

"I've been looking for a place to put down roots and I once met some people I took a real hankering to." He told Frank about the wagon train from Salt Lake to Tucson. "That's the kind of people I'd like to live and work among. I'm looking for a place where I'm needed but I don't think Buell is it."

"Needed!" Frank exploded. "Hell's fire! There's not a town in the Territory that needs a doc worse'n Buell. Holly Booth--she runs the rooming house across the street--is the only one in town to help the miners' wives with birthin', and when men got hurt in the mine Charlie Ivey used to patch 'em up--Charlie ran the barbershop and the pool hall. Last winter when the flu hit, half the people were down with it and most of them wound up in the cemetery because they got no doctorin'. One of 'em was Charlie Ivey, so we don't even have him now. Tom Pender visited every town within fifty miles tryin' to get a doctor to come."

As Frank talked, Opal stared at him a moment then ran into the other room. Frank lowered his voice. "We lost our youngest during the sickness; he wasn't quite a year old. I was in Tucson on a buying trip and Opal was alone with Danny and our daughter, Nan. The thing hit so fast; people would take sick and run a high fever untill finally it seemed they couldn't get air through their windpipes and they died. Little Danny lived less than an hour after I got home. His death seems to have done somethin' permanent to Opal. She's been like you seen her all the time. I've even thought of takin' her outta this town, but I don't think it would change anything. So, if it's needin' you're wantin', Doc, you're sure as hell needed right here!"

Doc stared at the cloud of cigar smoke for a moment. "I'll mull it over for a while." Changing the subject, he contunued, "This fellow Tom Pender. I remember hearing mention of him in Tucson and if I recollect the story right, he was laying for someone. How'd he happen to wind up in Buell?"

Frank settled back in his chair. "Tom mentioned he landed in Tucson to sign on for a cattle drive, but White and Beasley offered him a better deal to wrangle their remuda of work horses. Tom's a funny one, but then, who ain't in this Godforsaken town? Everybody here, and that includes me I guess, is chewin' on a hunk of bile.

"Speakin' of Tom, I think you heard right about him gunnin' for some jasper. Every mornin' he goes down the wash below the bridge and blasts away with his gun and it's always twelve shots, never more, never less. You be here tomorrow mornin' and you'll hear an even dozen. It's been like that ever since he hit town. He's keepin' his draw sharp for some reason. If you're a mind to, we can meet Tom and some of the others at the China Girl tonight.

"Henry Powell, our blacksmith, will be there. You can meet him, but Henry ain't much for visitin. Jed, the bartender at the China Girl, is a pretty decent guy, which almost makes him a misfit in this town. Dolph Edelblute'll be there; he runs the harness and gun shop. Folks say Dolph once owned one of the best spreads in Montana and lost it in an all-night poker game. Dolph'll bet on anything."

"Asa Perth'll likely stop by. He runs the mining company's assay office. He'll take thirty minutes drinkin' two whiskeys and after he's finished with the second one, he'll say, like he always does to whoever's standin' near him, "Friend, do you think the hen can outrun the rooster?' Then he'll stick his fingers in his vest pockets, chuckle to himself an' walk out. It's a regular evenin' ritual with Asa.

"Some of the miners'll drop by an' if Red Heyden is with 'em there'll be a fist fight. Red's foreman at the mine and a fight in the saloon is his way of remindin' the men who's boss. Anyway, Red'ud rather fight than drink and he does a tol'able good job at both."

"Frank," Doc said, "it sounds most interesting. If Mrs. Booth has a room for me, I've a mind to stay over a day or two."

Doc drove his team to the livery stable. Henry was working under the lean'to he used as a blacksmith shop. The ring of the hammer on steel was deafening and Doc's loud call of "howdy!" did not penetrate the wall of sound. Finally, he walked around in front of Henry to get his attention.

Henry wore a leather apron that molded his chest and torso. His bare arms glistened with sweat and his cheek bulged with a cud of tobacco. He had an agreement with the mining company to keep their horses shod and the rolling stock repaired, so he had no time for idle talk. When he saw Doc, he bathed a nearby post with tobacco juice and grunted, "Wantin' somethin'?"

"Wanting to put my team up for a couple of days," said Doc, a little irritated by the brusque question.

"A dollar a day with hay," Henry said. "Fifty cents more for grain."

"Sounds reasonable," Doc said.

"One day in advance," Henry added.

Doc dug up a dollar and a half and handed it to the blacksmith. "I'm Doc Jarka and I"m staying at Booth's place."

All but the first word or two were drowned in the clanging of Henry's hammer resumed. Doc stood waiting. "Well?" Henry asked.

"You're holding a dollar and a half of my money to care for my team," said Doc. "I'd kind of like to see you start the caring."

Henry struck one more ringing blow, then dropped the hammer and headed for the team.

Doc had his evening meal with Holly and her guests, then strolled across to the China Girl. Frank came in shortly after and joined him at the bar. By ones and twos the men drifted into the saloon and Frank introduced them as they arrived. Doc was just telling Frank of his encounter with the blacksmith when Henry walked in. Jed set a bottle in front of his newest customer and Henry lifted it to his mouth. When he put it down it was half empty.

"Whoo-ee!" said Doc in a low voice. "There's a man with a thirst!"

Some of the miners started a poker game and others kept up a steady pace of bending their elbows at the bar. Doc spotted the redhead among them and pointed with his thumb. Frank nodded. "That's him," he said.

"He's sporting a generous amount of muscle," Doc observed.

"Folks here have been waitin' for him and Henry to tangle. Be quite a tussle, I'm thinkin'. Red's willin' and he's tried to get Henry riled up two or three times, but Henry pays him no mind."

Frank wandered away to visit with one of the miners and Doc and Jed continued talking. Suddenly, Doc heard someone say, "Friend, you reckon the hen can outrun the rooster?" He looked and saw a small man with steel-rimmed glasses and a derby hat leave the bar and head for the door.

While he was chuckling over the predictable little man, he heard the sound of a fist hitting flesh. He turned in time to see the second punch uncorked as Red waded into his first fight of the night.

"Time to leave," Doc said. "I'll see you tomorrow, Jed." He turned to leave. "You sure got this town pegged and pickled," he said to Frank on his way out.

Doc decided to stay in Buell and arranged to have medical supplies and his equipment brought from Tucson. There was a vacant building directly across from

Applegate's store, formerly the mining company office before they moved to a new building at the other end of town. Within three weeks, he had his supplies and his office was open for business. He nailed a board to a post out front, freshly painted with his name, S.E. Jarka, M.D. This morning, he tacked a note on the front door which read, "Call at the China Girl," and strolled to the saloon for a beer and a visit with Jed.

Although Doc had not been in town long, he knew the lone figure at the bar was a stranger. He was dressed in black and wore his gun low on the hip. the man studied Doc in the mirror behind the bar, decided he was harmless and returned to his drink. Jed drew a mug of beer and met Doc at the end of the bar.

"I'm ready for business, Jed, and I figured you could help me spread the word. Got my knife sharpened, a few spools of catgut and about a half ton of pills all ready," Doc greeted.

The man at the bar looked up. "How're ya fixed for plugs?"

"Plugs?" Doc asked.

"Plugs," the gunman repeated and tossed down his drink. "I'm figerrin' to put a hole through one a your good citizens and might be he'll be wantin' ya to plug it."

Doc was at a loss for an answer. He looked carefully at the speaker, who stared back, his smokey eyes sending a chill down Doc's back. The gunman shoved his glass toward Jed for a refill. "You got a loud-mouth holed up here that's been spoutin' off for quite a spell that he was lookin' for Will Storms?" He downed his drink and put the glass on the bar. "I'm Will Storms."

Silence hung heavy in the room for a few moments and when neither Doc nor Jed responded to his announcement, he spoke again. "Ain't you interested in who I'm gunnin' for?" he asked Jed.

"It's your business Mister. I just pour booze and beer," Jed replied.

The man shifted his attention to Doc. "Tell us," Doc said. "I expect you're going to anyway." Doc suddenly remembered the ritual of twelve shots he heard this morning and was not surprised at the man's answer.

"Tom Pender; a sniveling, yellow-bellied, butter-kneed kid with a loud mouth by the name of Tom Pender."

Halfway through the sentence, the front door opened and a man walked in. "Did I hear my name?" he asked.

The man at the bar grew rigid, then very slowly he straightened and turned. Tom walked to the end of the bar beside Doc. When he got a good look at the gunman, he said, "Welcome to Buell, bad man."

Will took a careful step away from the bar. "Word is, you been lookin' for me."

Tom stepped into the clear and the two men stood facing each other about fifteen feet apart. "That's right, Storms, I've been looking for you. I got something I want to give you and I'm gonna put it right through your left shirt pocket."

"Somebody's been teachin' you some mighty big talk," said Will.

"Right again," Tom answered. "Old friend of yours taught me a number of things; fella named Crimp Madsen."

"I could take Crimp the best day he ever lived," Will boasted.

"Crimp says I'm a right smart faster than he ever was."

"'Pears to me you're plannin' on talkin' me to death," Will taunted.

"Doc," said Tom, "lift my gun out and lay it on the bar."

"What the hell's goin' on?" Will growled.

Tom ignored the question. "Now, take out the shells," he instructed and Doc did as he was told.

"There's a bullet in my right-hand shirt pocket; lift it out." Again Doc did as he was told and held the forty-five slug between his fingers. "I been carryin' this for a long, long time," Tom said. "I took it from the belt of the man you gunned in a saloon in Prattsville one night, and if you look close you'll see I scratched your name on it. Put the shell in the chamber next to the hammer, Doc, and drop the gun back in my holster." When this was done

Tom continued, "All right, bad man, whenever you're ready."

Will leaned into a crouch. "You're the one with the big mouth; make your move."

"Doc," said Tom, "light a cigar." Then to Will, "We'll go with the scratch of the match."

Doc was mesmerized by the scene as he moved to follow Tom's order. He dug in his vest for a cigar, bit off the end, and placed it in his mouth. The two men stood motionless and the ticking of the wall clock bounced around the room. Doc searched for a match. When he found one, he struck it against the edge of the table where he now stood.

Before it flared into flame, the room was filled with the thunder of gunfire. Doc held the match in mid-air and saw that both men stood just as before. Then, very slowly, Will Storms pitched forward on his face. Tom broke his gun open and started reloading the cartridges on the bar, ordering a whiskey as he did so.

Doc walked to the fallen man and rolled him over on his back. He saw the hole through the left vest pocket and knew the gunman was dead. Doc also noticed that Will's gun was still in its holster.

Tom rolled the empty casing he had just taken from his gun back and forth in the palm of his hand. He looked at it a moment, then walked over and dropped it on the body on the floor.

While Jed poured his whiskey, Tom walked behind the bar, unbuckling his gunbelt as he went. A set of antlers was fastened to the wall there and Tom hung his gun and belt on them. He returned to his whiskey, drained the glass and headed for the door.

He met Frank Applegate coming in. Frank started to speak, but Tom interrupted him. "Jed'll tell you the whole story." He brushed past and walked to the hitching rail, mounted his horse and road toward the mine.

128

CHAPTER FIFTEEN
The First Death of Tom Pender

The shooting in the China Girl revived the talk that Buell should have a marshal, so the businessmen of the town gathered at Applegate's store one Sunday evening and Frank took the floor. "Men," he began, "it appears to me it's time this town had a little organization. I've talked to most of you separately, and you agree we need a town council and a marshal. We need laws and someone to enforce them; this is our most pressin' problem. If we get this settled, then we got to put our minds to the other problems of the town.

"First off, we're forming a citizens' committee and every man here is a member. The duties of this committee are to write a charter and appoint a temporary mayor and council until we can hold an election. Bein's Doc has a right smart more education than me, I'm gonna appoint him chairman of this committee. Doc, take the floor."

The meeting ran until after midnight and some progress was made. Finally, Doc adjourned the meeting with instructions to talk it over among themselves and meet again in one week.

The attendance at the second meeting dropped nearly fifty percent and Doc and Frank were angered by the apparent loss of interest. Doc called the meeting to order and made the steaming speech with instructions for the men present to carry his opinions to the other businessmen in town. "Get out and tell your neighbors how important these meetings are. There'll be another one in a week. Tell them to get their butts back here and attend it!"

The third and last meeting of the Buell Businessmen's Committee had an attendance of four: Doc, Frank, Jed and Asa Perth. After looking at his watch for the fifth time, Doc said. "Well, that's that. It seems Buell won't have a mayor or a council or a marshal. I guess it'll take a calamity to wake them up."

"The hell with them!" said the angry Frank. "Let's go have a beer."

Doc looked over at Asa, who was sitting with his hand raised. "For the love of Pete, Asa! There's no meeting going on; you want to say something, say it!"

Asa stood and cleared his throat. "I want to report to the committee..."

"Thunderation!" Frank interrupted. "Report to what committee? There ain't no committee, you little twerp!"

Asa kept his composure and when Frank had finished, he continued, "...that the company intends to construct a schoolhouse, with supplies and furnishings, and will also employ a teacher. Thank you." He sat down again.

"Asa, that's great news!" Doc exclaimed. "Isn't that great news, Jed? Frank?" Doc's question left Frank with his head bowed in embarrassment. He had taken out his anger at the others on Asa and now was searching for a way to get his foot out of his mouth.

"The mine's been taking long enough. About time they gave a little," Jed remarked caustically.

Doc was so delighted he walked over to shake hands with he little man. "Asa, I don't really know what to say. I think the company's doing a fine thing for the town. My final act as temporary chairman of the Citizens' Committee will be to write a letter of appreciation to the president of the White and Beasley Mining Company. Now, can I buy you a beer?" Asa nodded his agreement and Doc said, "I declare this meeting adjourned."

As they went out the door, Frank put his arm around Asa's shoulder and said, "Asa, I think we made progress tonight and I thank you."

True to their promise, the mining company put some men to work building the schoolhouse. A site was chosen on a knoll about halfway between the cluster of miner's homes and the business section of Buell, and with an abundance of men available the building went up rapidly. By the time the roof was completed, the second coat of red paint was being applied and white shutters were installed at the windows. As the front door was being hung, the wagon arrived with a potbellied stove, the children's benches and the teacher's desk. The following Sunday was chosen as the day of dedication, and Millard Corwin, Sr., president of the White and Beasley Mining Company, was to make the dedication speech.

It was the last Sunday in August and the Arizona weather was at its best. The turnout surprised even Mr. Corwin. The miners and their wives and children showed up to inspect and admire the new schoolhouse, then the mothers stopped by Mr. Corwin's surrey to thank him and the company for the good thing they had done. The impeccably dressed Mr. Corwin tipped his hat and smiled broadly at the sunbonneted ladies.

Then, to everyone's amazement, lunch baskets appeared, filled with fried chicken, pots of baked beans and a variety of cakes. There was a fiddler, then another, then a guitar and a mouth organ and the music started. Almost better than if it had been planned, a square dance got under way on the level spot in front of the school.

Jed had left the relief bartender at the China Girl and joined Doc for the stroll to the schoolhouse. When he saw the celebration that was forming, he walked over and had a few words with Mr. Corwin, then climbed into the surrey with him and headed into town. In a short time they were back with a barrel of beer and mugs for the men. Frank Applegate witnessed this from the edge of the crowd, and not to be outdone, he and two of the miners went down the hill and returned with two boxes of assorted candy for the children. The candy drew them like ants and soon each child had a peppermint or cinnamon stick protruding from his or her mouth, with a reserve of licorice drops and fruit balls in a pocket.

Doc took a seat on the schoolhouse steps and smoked a cigar, taking in the scene before him; the musicians and the dancers, the picnic baskets and candy boxes, and the miners lined up for beer. "I'll be damned," he said to himself. "This place just might become a town after all." The laughter he heard was more musical to him than the music itself. But something nagged at his mind, and then it finally came to him. I must plant Mary Harvey's rose tomorrow, he thought.

During a lull between dance sets a spring wagon arrived from the direction of the mine office carrying an object covered with a tarpaulin. It stopped in front of the schoolhouse door and Mr. Corwin climbed into the wagon bed, hands held up for attention, and started his dedicatory speech. The crowd gathered around.

"Citizens of Buell. As president of White and Beasley Mining Company, it is my pleasure to welcome you here this afternoon for the dedication of this schoolhouse. As you know, the company is furnishing it with all the necessary equipment to operate a first-class school. That includes books, a blackboard, a four-by-six map of America and even a flag with a staff and base. I am also pleased to announce that we have been able to engage a schoolmistress. Her name is Marguerite Penhorwood and she will be arriving by stage in a few days. The company proposes to pay her salary for one year, then it will be the town's responsibility. I have a key to the door which I'm going to turn over to Frank Applegate to hold until Miss Penhorwood arrives.

"The company is very pleased to have this opportunity to contribute to the community and joins me in the sincere hope that some of the future leaders of America will receive their education in this schoolhouse. There now remains but one final thing to be taken care of."

While he had been talking, the driver of the wagon had carried the covered object to the small porch by the front door of the schoolhouse. Mr. Corwin now left the wagon and walked up the steps. "It is my thought that you cannot have a school without a bell."

So saying, he removed the tarpaulin and revealed a bronze bell with the name Buell inlaid in silver. "The silver in the lettering is from our mine, the bell is my personal contribution. It will be mounted in the bell tower, and if all goes well it will ring for the first time on the morning of the first Monday in September to announce that school is open." He descended the steps amid cheers and applause.

Doc stood to the side, watching, and for the second time within an hour he murmured, "Well, I'll be damned!"

Doc was heading across the street to the store for a supply of cigars when he was met by little Nan Applegate, who took his hand and walked beside him.

"Today's my birthday, Doc," she said. "I'm eight years old and Mommie's baking a cake for me. I'm gonna have a party and you're invited."

"Well, little miss eight-year old," he said as he swung her up into his arms. "I guess this does call for a celebration."

"Mommie said we could have a picnic today at the canyon, but we're gonna have our party inside 'cause Daddy said it's gonna rain."

He glanced up and saw a sky filled with white puffballs of clouds. "Your Daddy's hollering out the wrong window; it's not going to rain."

"But look at all those clouds!" the little girl exclaimed.

"I know honey, but those are not rain clouds. They're cowboys who have died and gone to heaven."

"Aw Doc, you're spoofin' me," said Nan.

"No I'm not, princess. You see, it's like this. When cowboys are alive and on earth they spend so much time on the hot, dry range hoping and sometimes praying for rain that when they die they go to heaven and become little white clouds. Then they spend their time rounding up rain clouds to bring rain to their cowboy buddies left out on the range. That's what they're doing now. It'll probably rain tomorrow, but not today."

They stopped in the middle of the street while Nan studied the puffs in the sky. Doc looked at her, but whether she believed him or not he couldn't tell.

They were both so engrossed with the story that neither heard the stranger ride up. When Doc became aware of the man's presence, he turned and said, "Howdy!"

The sinister-looking character on the black horse ignored his greeting. "I hear you got a fast gun in town by the name of Tom Pender."

Doc gave Nan a pat and headed her toward her father's store. "There's a fellow lives here by that name of Tom Pender, but he doesn't wear a gun, so most likely he's not the Pender you're looking for."

"He's the one, all right. He gunned down Will Storms. You see him, tell him Biff Devlyn'd like to try him on fer size. Tell him I'll be waitin' at the saloon and I don't wait good." He wheeled his horse and rode away.

Doc watched him ride off and thought, that may just be the calamity I said would wake-up this town, but I hate to see it come. He headed for the store to tell Frank about this latest development.

As he reached the porch, he heard the sound of a horse approaching from the direction of the corral. It was Tom Pender. He waited and as Tom drew abreast he called out. "There's a hardcase just hit town, mean-looking fella who calls himself Biff Devlyn. He extended an invitation for you to meet him at the China Girl. It would appear to me that what he has in mind is a shootout."

Tom made no answer. Instead, he sat quietly on his horse and stared off in the direction of the saloon.

Doc continued. "If you were to ride out to Bisbee or Tucson or somewhere for a few days, I'm sure this gunslinger would get tired of waiting and head elsewhere."

"No, Doc, it won't work. There'd be another one after him and another after that. If I can convince this jasper I'm through with guns, maybe he'll spread the word and it'll end before it gets started. I gotta see him, there's ain't no doubt about that, but first I got some business with Mister Perth for the mine, then I'll drop by for a visit with Mister Devlyn."

Late that afternoon Tom walked into the China Girl and headed for his favorite spot at the end of the bar. Standing at the other end was a man playing solitaire with a deck of grimy cards. Besides Jed, he was the only man there. Jed was filling lamps for the evening's business. When he saw Tom, he held up a beer mug and Tom nodded. Jed proceeded to draw him a glass of beer.

The man at the bar dropped the deck of cards and turned to study Tom carefully. "I got a strong notion yer Tom Pender," he drawled.

Tom drained half his beer and put the glass on the bar. "Your notion is correct," he replied.

"Talk is yer the fast gun what dropped Will Storms."

"Right again. He died in the exact spot where you're standin'."

"If you downed Will you must be real fast. I'm gonna find out how fast."

"You'll never know," Tom said. "If you look on the wall behind the bar you'll see my gun. I hung it there and there it's gonna stay." Even as he spoke, he felt the twitch in the palm of his hand and the nerves tingled in his arm with the desire to match speed with the man facing him. It was just as Crimp had said it would be.

Biff stepped away from the bar. "There's a half dozen ways a makin' you strap that gun on, Mister, and one way or 'nother yer gonna do it."

"You plannin' on spittin' in my eye or callin' me yella? If that's what you're thinkin', it won't work. I gave Will Storms what he deserved, then I took my gun off and it's gonna stay off. And there ain't nothin' that you or a dozen like you can say or do that'll change that, so ride outta here and look for a fast gun in some other town 'cause there ain't none in Buell."

Biff walked behind Tom and around the end of the bar and lifted the gun and belt from the wall. Then he walked back to his original position and placed the gunbelt on the bar, sliding it down to Tom. "Fer the last time," he said, "strap it on!"

"Go to hell!" was Tom's answer.

Biff stood for a moment watching Tom finish his beer. Then he tried another tack. "I noticed ridin' inta town you have a nice new schoolhouse on the hill out back. Ever since I was a little kid I've had a powerful dislike for schoolhouses. Barkeep, pass over one a those lamps you was fillin'; all that new lumber and fresh paint oughtta make a right nice fire. And just so I don't git back-shot, you walk out ahead a me barkeep, out the back door, slow and easy-like, and head fer the schoolhouse. I'll be right behind you and if you as much as stumble, I'll blow yer head off!"

Jed was trouble-wise enough to know that the gun-crazy man had to be obeyed until something could be figured out. As they went out the door, Biff turned and said to Tom, "You got about one minute to strap that gun on, or come outside an' watch one helluva fire."

Tom was shocked by the insane audacity of the man. From where he stood he could see the two men climbing the short distance to the schoolhouse. Biff stopped by a window, dug in his pocket for a match and struck it on his pant leg. He was holding it to the wick of the lamp when Tom reached for the gun on the bar.

Biff saw him coming and handed the lighted lamp to Jed. About forty feet from the gunman, Tom stopped to tie the holster thongs above his knee. "I had no reason before," he said, "but now you have given me one. 'Pears you crawled out of the same rathole as Will."

Biff stood still, only moving his hand into position, and as the seconds passed Tom knew he was keeping his nerves pitched to their highest tune just before the draw. He knew because he was doing the same. The thrill was there, there was no denying it. His arm tingled, his blood raced, and the excitement was almost ecstasy. In another split second there would be ten inches of flame and a little black hole would pop out on Biff's shirt front.

The roar of the shot was thunderous. Biff's knees buckled and he dropped to the ground, his fingers having barely touched his gun butt. It was another split second before Tom realized that he hadn't made the draw; his gun was still in its holster.

His senses told him that the sound he had heard could only have come from a rifle. He looked to his left and a little behind him to where a man sat on a horse, sliding a Winchester back into its scabbard. He spurred the horse to a slow walk and when he reached Tom he said, "Sorry 'bout that, but maybe this'll explain it." He handed Tom a poster that read, "Wanted for murder, Biff Devlyn, one thousand dollars reward, dead or alive."

Tom looked up and watched the stranger light a small, black cigar. "Who are you, Mister?"

"Harp, I'm called. I'm a bounty hunter. I knew Devlyn would never be taken alive anyway, so I figgered I might as well do the shootin' since I was gettin' paid for it."

"I'm obliged to you," Tom said, but with little conviction. He felt cheated; the question of whether or not he was faster than Devlyn would never be answered now. He drew an X in the dust of the street with the toe of his boot and studied it for a moment. "Reckon it's a little light on the beam scale," he said, "but I'd be right pleased to buy the drinks."

"You can deal me in that hand," Harp said, "but first I got some things to take care of. I need to see your marshal, then..."

"We got no marshal," Tom interrupted, "but the mine has a telegraph to Bisbee; you could reach the sheriff there."

Harp looked up and down the main street of town. "No marshal," he said. "You all better do somethin' 'bout that, friend, or you'll have another Gayleville here 'bouts. Gayleville's got more varmints than a woodpile and gettin' worse ever' day." Turning back to Tom he said, "You got a livery here? The other thing I wanted to take care of was gettin' some feed for my horse before I pull out."

"The livery's at the other end of town. I'll walk with you and introduce you to the man that runs it, name of Henry Powell."

Harp stood still. "Henry Powell," he said. "I knew a fella by that name once. Just a kid, but a mighty big one. Back in Missouri or Kansas, if I recollect. Long time ago, it was. Likely it ain't the same fella I knew."

Henry was dipping a red-hot shoe into a tank of water when Tom and Harp walked up. He paid little attention to them, but a short study of the blacksmith's face let Harp know that, although the change was great, he was the man who had buffaloed him one morning years ago near a grove of cottonwood outside Jefferson City, Missouri.

Henry hung the tempered shoe on a wire with a couple dozen others, then turned to face his visitors. Harp was astonished by the change in the man's features. There was a look about him somewhere between defiance and fear, accentuated by eyes that did not blink but bored into anything they touched and his lips were so tightly compressed that his jaw muscles bulged; his smoke-darkened face reflected more years than he could possibly have lived.

"Henry," Tom began, "this here is Harp..." Turning to his companion, he said, "I didn't get your last name."

"Didn't give it," said Harp.

Henry took a couple of steps forward and recognition appeared in his eyes. "The bounty hunter!" he said. "I thought about you many a time through the years; wonder' did you make out all right with that busted leg."

"Old Doc fixed me up fine. But you," Harp said, "I've wondered what trail you cut. What you been doin' all these years? Did you make it to California? How did you come to wind up in this burg?" Henry seemed to be studying which question to answer first. "And what about Chalkie?" Harp continued. "Could it be you still got him?"

"Chalkie?" Henry asked, puzzled.

"My Appaloosa you rode away on that day; I called him Chalkie."

Henry's answer was slow coming. "No. He's gone. Indians...Yellow Wolf."

A look of pain crossed Henry's face and Harp knew he had touched an unhealed wound so he decided to change the subject. "Tom, if that invite still holds, let's all go get on the outside of some good drinkin' liquor. Henry and I got a right smart of visitin' to do and there's nothin' like good rye whiskey when a body has a mind to do some visitin'."

There have been some memorable drinking matches in the Old West--Doc Holiday and Johnnie Ringo in Tombstone; Ben Thompson and Jack Kellman in Silver City; Bat Masterson and Jake O'Day in Dodge City; Jim Quinn and Johnny Benton in Bitterroot--but the one that August afternoon in the China Girl Saloon in Buell, Arizona Territory, was to outdo them all.

Henry and Harp drank and visited while Tom just drank. There is almost always one exceptionally wild fling in every man's destiny and it usually besets him without warning; this was Tom's. Later in the afternoon, the miners began to drift in and by evening two poker tables were going strong and the room was filled with smoke.

A new bartender who called himself Squint had been hired that day to assist Jed and the two were kept busy. Flo, the barmaid, was serving drinks with one hand

and slapping away pats from the miners with the other.

A considerable quantity of rye had loosened Henry's tongue and he was recounting the events of the past ten years to Harp. They stood at one end of the bar and Tom held down his favorite spot at the other. The more liquor he drank, the sweeter it tasted and the drinks began to come more often. By dark he was gloriously drunk. Hat-waving, song-singing drunk. He bought drinks for the house and went down the line, lying and laughing with each of the men standing there. He wove his way among the tables until he had shaken the hand and slapped the back of everyone in the place. He drank from every bottle offered him and some that weren't and he kibitzed at the poker table until he was cussed out. Then he staggered off laughing and bumped headlong into Flo, knocking the tray of beer mugs she was carrying to the floor. He made a big thing of telling her how sorry he was and tried to help her clean up the mess, then he staggered to the bar and got another trayful to replace the one he had knocked out of her hands. He was balancing it carefully on both palms when he tripped over his own feet and fell headlong into the first mess he had made.

The saloon roared with laughter and when Tom got up, pleased that he had furnished them with some entertainment, he attempted a bow and nearly fell again. Flo retrieved his hat from the floor and jammed it into his hands, shoving him toward Henry and Harp. He bumped Harp hard. "'Lo," he said. "I think I'm li'l drunk."

"I don't know how you figger that," Harp said. "You only drunk half the booze in the place, fell down twice, and nearly got yourself thrown out. Don't see why..."

"Just hol' it a dern minute," Tom interrupted. "I bin watchin' you 'n Henry pourin' it in like you had a hole in yer boot."

"Yeah," said Harp, "but Henry an' me knows how to drink. We don't turn into songbirds and toe dancers and fall over our own feet."

"Now jis' a minute," Tom protested. "I can out-fight, out-love, out-ride, 'n out-drink you 'n Henry 'n ten more like ya."

"Now that's an interestin' remark," Harp said, "and seein' as how yer gonna make this your night to howl, let's just see how wild a coyote you are. I ain't a lover and I do my fightin' with a gun, so that leaves drinkin' and ridin'."

"Name yer game," said Tom, taking a heist at his belt.

"Barkeep," said Harp, "set four bottles of rye on the bar." Turning back to Tom he continued. "First off, I don't do anything for nothin'. If you got twenty dollars gold you're willin' to wager, toss it on the bar."

"Done," Tom said and complied. "Now, if you wouldn' mind lettin' me in on what this contest is, I'll beat ya at yer own game."

"We're gonna do some drinkin' then some ridin', then some more drinkin'; the first one through picks up the forty. When I rode in this mornin', I spotted a mine wagon that slid off the road 'bout five miles back. Now, here's the riffle. At a signal from the barkeep, we each start on a bottle of rye. When it's empty, we mount up, ride to the wagon, make our mark, then ride back and finish off the second bottle. The first man with both bottles empty'll be declared the winner by the barkeep."

Tom let out a cry of exultation and slapped Harp on the shoulder. "You got yerself a bet," he said. "I'll likely have a nip 'r two outta my saddlebag on the way."

The word spread among the men at the tables and they gathered around to watch. Tom grabbed a bottle and pulled the cork. "Make the signal, Jed." He turned to the crowd. "Open up a path there, men, or in 'bout a minute this grizzly'll tromp ya down."

"GO!" Jed shouted, and the gurgling began.

Tom gulped and gasped and slopped whiskey down the front of his shirt, squinching his eyes against the fumes. Harp drank slower, but steadily, and they finished almost together. Tom made a weaving run for the door while Harp walked. Jed heard Tom's horse break into a gallop, followed an instant later by Harp's.

He turned to Dolph. "I think we'll need Doc before this night's over," he commented. He glanced at the two bottles left sitting on the bar and shook his head.

They were still sitting there when the sun came up the next morning.

It was unusually quiet in Buell on the morning of August 28, 1878. The birds and chipmunks and a rabbit or two were busy with early morning capers. The town seemed to have overslept. The sun crept up Cayente Canyon, pushing the shadows and coolness ahead of it. When Doc stepped out of Holly's boarding house and trudged toward his office, the sweetness of the departing night air added to the peaceful scene. There was nothing to indicate that it would be a bad day for Buell.

Doc was thinking of the fun he had had at little Nan's birthday party when he heard a horse coming into town. He turned and, recognizing Tom Pender, he waved a greeting and went into his office.

Tom's horse stopped in front of the China Girl and he slid to the ground, making his way unsteadily to the door. Jed was just tying on his apron as Tom walked in. "Holy Mother of Moses!" he said. "If you don't look like what fell outta the wagon! Where's the sidekick you went gallopin' off with last night?"

"You mean Harp?" said Tom. "I'm a little fuzzy on that, but I seem to recollect he said somethin' about headin' to Tucson. Had a hankerin' to see some gal name of Violet.

"Now, please, no talkin' for a while. Just help me stop this sledgehammer poundin' the top of my head. Pour me a little 'hair of the dog'. If I can use your back room I'd like to slosh some cold water on my face."

"Help yourself," said Jed as he set up a glass and reached for a bottle.

Outside, Tom's horse stood with its head down, half-heartedly switching its tail at the annoying flies. The next sound to intrude on the morning was that of a window being raised above Applegate's store as Frank's head emerged to take a look at the new day. From down the street came the squeak of a pump, followed by the slamming of a door. The town of Buell was waking up.

Suddenly, the tranquility was shattered by the pounding hooves of a galloping horse and the shrill shouts of its rider. Frank watched from his window and as the horse approached the livery stable, he saw Henry run to the center of the street and grab the reins of the galloping horse, dragging it to a stop.

In a minute or two, a group had gathered around the excited man. Frank and Doc got there first, then Dolph and his clerk, Emery. One by one, others appeared. the man was almost incoherent in his excitement, but Doc finally got him to calm down enough to tell his story.

His name was Shelly Owen and he and his wife Ruth had been on their way to Buell when night came upon them and they had pulled their wagon into an arroyo until morning. They had been asleep in the wagon when they were awakened by loud talk from two men who had ridden into their camp. Shelly had gotten up to investigate when one of the strangers threw a rope over his shoulders and pulled him to the ground. While the second rider laughed, the first one had dragged him several yards then dismounted and tied him to a tree.

His wife, clad in night clothes, had appeared at the open end of the wagon to see what was happening when one of the men rode up, pulled her onto the horse in front of him, and with much yelling and laughing, rode off with her.

Shelly had struggled for what seemed hours to free himself; then he had ridden off in the direction the two men had taken. He did not know how long he had ridden in the darkness trying to find a trail when he finally came upon a road and decided to ride for help, and here he was.

That was his story and after telling it, he covered his face with his hands.

Doc led the distraught man to his office. Frank called to a few men in the crowd and soon had a posse together. Within minutes they were mounted and riding out of town.

The body of Ruth Owen was found two hours later in a clump of mesquite trees near Mica Springs. Her clothes were torn and disarranged and her throat was bruised and swollen. It was apparent that she had been strangled. Frank sent one of the riders back to bring the Owen wagon, then he dismounted and surveyed the scene.

He found horse tracks and the footprints of two men in the soft earth around the springs, but he missed those of a third man in the grass.

They took the body of the murdered woman to Doc's office. During the examination, he discovered that she had something clasped in one hand. When he pried it open he found a small white button.

Jed left Tom drinking with a drifter while he went to Doc's office to see what was going on. When he entered, Doc was staring at a button in the palm of his hand. Doc showed it to him and explained where he had found it. "We better send a rider to Bisbee for the sheriff," he said.

Doc looked over at the body of Mrs. Owen. "Maybe now we'll finally get some law in this town," he said.

"From the talk I heard on the way over here," said Jed, "the townspeople are pretty well worked up."

"With two shootings and now a murder, it's about time they got worked up," Doc answered.

"Who's this fella Owen?" Jed asked. "Anyone know anything about him?"

"They came in from Willcox. He's a barber and he planned on taking over Charlie Ivey's shop."

Jed shook his head in despair. "Sure beats hell," he said. "Well, I better get back to Tom. He's gettin liquored up again tryin' to pull outta his hangover. By the way, where is this fella Owen?"

"I sent him to the boarding house for coffee," Doc answered.

Jed had not taken a dozen steps when he heard a shout. Looking up the street, he saw a stranger whom he took to be Shelly Owen standing in front of the China Girl. "That's him!" the man was shouting. "That's the same voice and the same laugh I heard last night!" He started toward the saloon, but Jed caught him before he entered. Jed could hear Tom laughing inside. He grabbed the man by the arm. "Hold it, friend. What you so all-fired riled up about?"

"The man who killed my wife is in there!" he said.

"I'll never forget that laugh. It's him! I'm sure of it! Let me go!"

Jed pinned the man against the adobe wall. "Now you listen to me, Mister. Don't go bustin' into somethin' you might can't handle. You stay put and I'll look into this." He waited a moment until the man calmed down, then walked into the saloon and faced Tom.

Tom was holding a bottle of whiskey and laughing at some comment made by the drifter who slouched at a table. Tom's eyes finally focused on Jed. "Where in thunder is ever'one?" he asked. "Heard a commotion outside. What's goin' on?"

Jed took the bottle from him and looked him straight in the eyes. "Tom, you look like the dregs of hell. You're drunk and dirty and unshaven and..." his eyes dropped to Tom's shirt front as he added, "you got a button missin'."

Shelly Owen followed Jed into the saloon and Frank Applegate came in shortly after. Word had spread fast as all the pieces began to fit. Feeling was running high and a hanging was in the making. The time had come for the occupants of Buell to purge themselves of a near-lifetime of resentments and injustices. No one bothered to think, for if they had they would have know it wasn't the man but the act of revenge they were about to commit that became their obsession.

Each of the odd collection of business people had some bitterness eating at his brain; from Holly Booth, who lost her handsome husband to a dancehall girl; to Frank Applegate, who lived with the shame of cowardice; to Dolph Edelblut, who gambled away his home and fortune; to Asa Perth, who spent a lifetime licking boots; to Henry Powell, who's dream began and ended in a few short days until his beautiful wife was butchered before his eyes; to Jed, who lost a hand while trying to save a friend. Even Doc for a taste of justice and the law and order that would bring him the peace and contentment he had yearned for so long. All sought to cleanse their souls and repair their dreams by tossing all their afflictions on the fire they would build to destroy the evil of one man among them, and in so doing, remove the evil that plagued them all.

Shelly Owen was shouting and raving for immediate action and their guilt concerning the fact that they had neglected to establish law and order was the reason they used to justify their actions. The true reason was the spot of darkness that lay within them all. Thus, with a sudden display of piety, a Citizen's Committee was formed and while Tom was held under guard the Committee discussed the matter. They decided that a quick exhibition of civil justice would make up for years of none. After all, Tom was guilty because he had to be guilty, Shelly Owen said he was, the missing button said he was. Anyway, it wasn't the man they were about to execute but the execution itself that counted.

Since there was no courtroom or magistrate's office, it was decided that the trial would be held at the foot of Main Street near the bridge. With the thought of making it as legal as possible, Asa brought an American flag from his office and Holly Booth brought a Bible. Frank Applegate was chosen as judge and he and Tom were given chairs to sit in. All the rest, including the jury, stood.

The trial was over in less than an hour. Tom violently protested his innocence and although everyone listened, no one heard. The button was introduced as evidence and the whole thing was wrapped up tight and final with Shelly Owen's testimony.

The short-count jury's decision was quick in coming. Tom was caught between disbelief and panic. He looked at the faces around him and they were all familiar, but they were strangers now. He kept waiting for someone to break into laughter, revealing that the whole thing was a joke.

While the jury was conferring in low tones, Tom studied Shelly Owen. Why was the man lying? He had to find out, and quickly, if he wanted to save his neck. Yet, when he looked at the other faces around him, he read on each of them a look of commitment that appeared irrevocable.

When Henry Powell stepped forward to announce the jury's decision, the crowd grew quiet. A sudden breeze blew the flag away from the staff Asa was holding and the ripples ran along the surface and snapped off at the end. That was the only sound in the hot street until Henry began to speak.

"Frank, we took what we saw and heard here, run it through a time or two, and ground it pretty fine. And bein's we can't find anything to the contrary, we all voted guilty. We figure the prisoner should rightly be hung."

The announcement was followed by silence, as if no one knew quite what to do or say. Doc had been watching everything and he caught a small significant sign at the conclusion of Henry's speech. The breeze had stopped as quickly as it began and the flag settled against the staff, almost as if it were retreating in shame. Frank stood up and motioned Tom to do the same.

"Tom Pender, you have been tried and found guilty of murder by this jury, and by the authority of the people of Buell, Arizona Territory, I sentence you to hang by the neck until you are dead. Sentence is to be carried out immediately." Frank hesitated, then as if it would make everything all right he added, "And may God have mercy on your soul."

The unbelievable thing that had just happened sobered Tom up considerably. He shook his head vigorously, trying to make sense of the events of the last couple of hours. He tried to talk to those standing near him, but they turned and walked away. Finally, since no one would listen, he shouted loud enough for everyone to hear. "I didn't do this thing! I didn't kill anybody! This is crazy! Somebody's got to believe me!"

There are two fevers that anesthetize the human brain: gold fever and hanging fever. Buell was now beset by the latter. Tom was taken under guard to Ivey's deserted barbershop and just before they pushed him through the door he shouted defiantly to the empty street, "I DIDN'T DO IT!"

Frank sent a messenger with word that Tom was to be given anything he wanted, within reason. Tom's answer was, "I don't want anything except somebody with some damn sense that will listen to me." The execution was set for three o'clock, the messenger added. Tom heard the words but his mind wouldn't accept them. Such things just didn't happen. He clung to the belief that the mess would straighten itself out and he would ride the hell out of this damn town for good.

Like a butterfly sleeping on an adobe wall, the town of Buell lay immobile and soundless in the heat of the August sun. Now and then a bird stopped at Henry's watering trough for a drink then flew away. A dust devil ventured into the center of town, played a while, then darted up the canyon. When the shadow at the foot of the canyon wall started its daily journey toward town, Frank came out of the back room to join the group of men in the front of his store. He nodded to one of them and said, "It's time."

The man left to fetch Tom. As he walked up the street, he noticed that others were walking toward the bridge, the site that had been chosen for the hanging.

When Tom and his guard reached the foot of the bridge, he saw a man leading a horse into the wash and another he recognized as Dolph Edelblut fashioning a noose in the end of a rope attached to the bridge railing. Not until then was he convinced that they intended to go through with it. "Holy Mother of God!" he gasped. "Have you all gone crazy!"

There was an occasional glance his way, but most eyes were downcast, they were all sick with "hanging fever". As Tom was led down the bank to the bed of the wash, the incredulity of the proceedings numbed his mind to the point where he was practically helpless. His hands were tied behind his back and two men hoisted him to the back of the horse. Immediately, Dolph placed the noose over Tom's head. The moment had come; the needle was in and the pulsing artery of the crowd was awaiting its jolt of morphine. For just a second, Frank looked at Tom's pleading, terror-stricken face, and for just a second, he hesitated. Then his eyes dropped to Tom's shirt front and the spot where the button was missing.

"In the name of God, Frank, I swear I didn't..." Tom began.

There was a slapping sound and Tom slid backward off the rump of the horse. He felt his body swing in long, lazy arcs from the shade of the bridge and back into the hot sunlight. His brain turned to hot brass as if he were falling headlong into the sun.

    He swung slower and slower and finally came to a stop four feet above the ground.

CHAPTER SIXTEEN
The Second Death of Tom Pender

The awareness that he was still alive was more of a perplexity than a relief. The hastily-prepared noose had not slipped as it should have; the rope under his chin was crushing his throat and the knot at the back of his head threatened to cave in his skull, but he was still alive and he knew it.

After witnessing the town's first execution, the people of Buell turned and quietly made their way to their homes and places of business. The stillness surrounding the body of Tom Pender was interrupted only by the buzzing of the flies about his face and the sound of a shovel digging in the sandy gravel of the canyon floor--someone was digging his grave.

Tom was denied the blessing of unconsciousness; instead, he hung in paralyzed agony. The pain and torment that gripped his brain were beyond the screaming point, beyond human endurance to the edge of where sanity departs. Suddenly, he felt his body being lifted, then he dropped into a merciful pool of blackness and his pain was gone.

Henry cut Tom's body down and carried it the short distance up the canyon to the shallow grave. He picked up Tom's hat from under the bridge and, after a momentary study of the young man's twisted features, he dropped it over Tom's face and filled in the grave. The crunch of his boots faded away toward town. The first death and burial of Tom Pender was finished.

Who could deny that Tom had died? He had met death and survived it; he had been hanged by the neck and had felt unspeakable pain. In the infinitesimal part of a second, he had jerked free of death and now lay in his grave, his heart still beating, enough air seeping through the coarse gravel and rocks to keep him alive.

A full moon rose over the Dragoon Mountains and the sleeping town of Buell. Consciousness returned to Tom and he fought for his senses. With awareness of the weight pressing upon him, he remembered what had happened, and with a strength born of panic, he pushed away the earth that covered him and rolled out onto the canyon floor. As he rose to a sitting position and struggled to draw in breaths of cool night air, the realization of what had happened cleared his frantic mind. He struggled to his feet and gazed into the grave.

Filled with dizziness and nausea, he knelt to retrieve his hat then carefully humped the dirt back into place so the grave still appeared to hold its occupant. With pain coursing through his body--pain that was to be with him for many months--he staggered to his feet and looked through the mouth of the canyon, past the bridge to the town of Buell. A plan was beginning to form in his mind.

His first move was to get his horse and he staggered toward Powell's livery. A little later, he sat his horse on the road leading down the canyon and looked back at the sleeping town. "You bastards! You self-righteous bastards!" he cursed his executioners. "I'll be back soon with your receipt!"

He rode to the canyon floor and headed northwest to Tucson. As he topped a rise, he saw the outline of a town against the brightening sky to his left and determined it to be Tombstone. While his horse munched on mesquite, he sat and pondered. Then, having decided the kind of help he wanted would more likely be in Tucson, he continued on his chosen path. Tombstone was as wild and lawless as Buell; he was convinced both towns had erupted from Hell.

The exhilaration of Tom's hanging soon turned into a hangover for the town of Buell; the purification process hadn't panned out. A few doubts began to creep in and the pride they had expected would come from swift justice and the inauguration of law and order did not develop. The entire affair lay over the town like a sickness.

Dolph Edelblut put it in simple terms. "It's like sleeping with a harlot," he said. "It seems like a good idea at the time, but afterwards you're ashamed."

The weeks went by and the town continued to function. The ore wagons continued their trips in and out of town, the school bell rang in the morning and at noon, and with the coming of winter, a few babies were born. A man named Mose Moots moved in and reopened the barbershop. He stayed exactly one month, then closed. The night before he left, he confided to Frank that the town was too creepy for him. "I haven't seen a smile or heard a pleasant word since I arrived. I don't know what's gnawing on this town and I don't intend to stay around to find out."

The China Girl continued to do a flourishing business with the miners and teamsters. Shelly Owen spent nearly every day in the saloon and played poker by the hour. When he caught someone staring at him he became sullen and irritable. One night in mid-December, he walked up to the bar for a drink and said to Jed, "I been wonderin' why the hell somebody don't throw dirt over this town like they would anything else that's dead." Then, without waiting for an answer, he downed his drink and walked out. That was the last anyone ever saw of him.

With the coming of spring, the town began to show signs of improvement; at least it seemed better outwardly. The mines continued to hire men, and early in May, a Mexican lady and her daughter opened a cafe in an empty building just west of Doc's office called Rosita's. Jed had a great fondness for Mexican food and he became their first and best customer.

Saturday, June 20, 1879, was the day of accounting for the town of Buell. Jed had just eaten breakfast at Rosita's and was crossing the street to open the China Girl. His spirits were higher than they had been for some time because it was to be his last day in town. He had quietly sold his interest in the saloon to a man from Tucson and he intended to ride out the following day.

He caught movement out of the corner of his eyes and turned to see three men on horseback riding slowly into town. They were too far away to recognize, but he had an idea he would have some early morning business. With a sigh of resignation he entered the saloon.

A few minutes later he was a little surprised to see just two of them walk in. Glancing over his shoulder, he saw a horse tied up at Rosita's and he supposed one of the three had decided to eat breakfast instead of drinking it.

Jed studied the two men as they approached the bar. They looked as if they were from two different pastures. One was a tall, bulky individual, unclean and unshaven, with dull features. The other was of medium build and adorned in costly western garb. He wore a dark green shirt and a brown and white calfskin vest. His broad-brimmed dark brown hat sported a one-inch copper band inset with pieces of turquoise. His face was thin and angular, with high cheekbones and black, deep-set eyes. his hands were small but muscular and one of them stayed close to the pearl-handled revolver he wore low on his thigh.

The big man was Mort Middleton and the smaller was well-known throughout the southwest as Johnny Stryker, gunman. Mort had two desires in life; first, to have all the beer he could drink some day, and second, to stay as close to his hero Johnny as he could.

Johnny Stryker was a cousin of Curly Bill, the Tombstone bad man, as he was quick to tell you if he got the chance. The feature that disturbed many a gunman who faced Johnny was his eyes. They were so black they seemed to have no pupil and you wondered if he was looking at you or somewhere else. By the time you decided, you were dead; Johnny was lightning fast with a gun.

Once, when Mort and Johnny were out in the desert, they spotted a coiled rattler in the shade of a rock. Johnny dismounted and squatted down in front of the snake. Suddenly, his left hand flicked out in a blur and he grabbed the rattler just behind its head as it was striking. He held the snake up and locked stares with it for a few seconds, then he tossed it into the air. As it hit the ground, he fired and the snake's head disappeared in an eruption of blood and sand.

"You're Jed," said Johnny. The gunman tipped his hat back and placed both hands on the edge of the bar. Jed searched the faces of the two men and sorted through his memory trying to hang a name on them. By force of habit he reached for a bar towel and as he did Johnny placed the barrel of his sixgun over the edge of the bar. "Easy, friend," Johnny said.

Jed did not speak, but he slowly brought his hand into plain view.

"Mort and I have a twenty-mile thirst so let's get to work on it. Mort's a beer drinker. Pass me over a bottle of rye," Johnny continued. While Jed set about filling the order, he asked, "Are you acquainted with a man hereabouts by the name of Frank Applegate?"

"Operates the general store next door," Jed answered.

"Get him over here," said Johnny.

Jed had served the drinks and stood looking at the two men before him.

"I mean now, friend!" the gunman added.

The order did not disturb Jed much for he had seen touchy gunhands before. However, he walked to the side door of the China Girl, crossed the narrow opening between the buildings and spoke to Opal through the open door. "Ask Frank if he can come over; a couple men want to see 'him. And tell 'im to come right away." He returned in time to fill Mort's empty mug and as he put a full one back on the bar Frank walked in.

"Hello, dead man," said Johnny.

"What kind of talk is that?" Frank asked. "Who are you?"

"Have a beer," said Johnny.

Frank ignored the invitation and turned to Johnny. "What do you want to see me about? I've got a business to run, you know."

"Mister Applegate, I said have a beer," Johnny repeated.

Frank hadn't taken his eyes off the gunman, yet, suddenly there was a gun in Johnny's hand pointed straight at Frank's middle. Jed was watching and decided to deal himself in. He was angry and his words showed it.

"What's this all about?" he demanded. "Who in damnation are you to come in here throwing your weight around!" Neither Johnny nor Mort moved. "Give me some answers," he ordered, "or get the hell out!" Johnny started to swing his sixshooter toward Jed. "Hold it right there Mister," he said. "I've got a ten gauge shotgun under the bar with the muzzle about six inches from your belly and my finger's on the trigger. You make just one little wrong move and I'll blow your belt buckle through your backbone."

"Now," said Jed, "how about those answers?"

As Johnny poured whiskey into a glass, he said, "You'll get your answers, barkeep, and you, too, Mister Applegate, any minute now. I can't say you're going to like them, but you're going to get them. Tom Pender will give you your answers when he walks through the front door."

Jed lifted the shotgun and placed it lengthwise on the bar, then, leaning, closer to Johnny, he said, "You're dealin' off the wrong deck, Mister. Tom Pender is dead and buried. I saw his hangin' and his burial myself."

Johnny picked up the bottle and his glass, walked to the nearest table and sat down. He hooked his thumbs in his gunbelt, stretched his legs out in front of him and sat contemplating his fancy, stitched boots for a second or two.

"No, barkeep, you just think he's dead. And so does Mister Applegate, here, and old Doc and your blacksmith and all the rest of this rotten town who tried and hung him for a crime he didn't do. Tom Pender is very much alive, as you'll soon see. You, Mister Applegate, were the almighty judge who pronounced sentence. Remember, Mister Applegate? Tom was alone through all of that but since then he's made some friends and we're here to help him square accounts. We rode in first to sort of set things up, but Tom'll be along."

Johnny got up and walked over to Frank, who was riveted to the floor. "Let Tom tell you, Mister Applegate, how it feels to hang and still live; how it feels to be suspended between life and death for what seems like an eternity. Let him tell you about the pain and the agony and about the sun cooking his brains. Listen to him tell you about the flies in his eyes and mouth and how it feels to be buried alive, Mister Applegate. And the panic he felt in his shallow grave. And all for a crime he didn't commit. It's taken him months to learn to talk again, and even now he sort of whispers through a crushed throat. But you'll be able to understand him. He doesn't look quite the same and his mind is a little twisted, but he remembers very well." Johnny walked back to the table and poured himself another drink.

Frank and Jed were frozen motionless, unable to believe what they had just heard. They needed more convincing and it was prompt in coming. Johnny directed his next words to Jed. "Didn't you people ever think about checking into Shelly Owen's back trail? Or wonder about his sudden departure from town? I don't suppose you know he was gunned down over a card game in Prescott three months ago, or that before he died he confessed to the Prescott marshal that he was the one who killed his wife."

Turning back to Frank, he continued, "Yes, Mister Applegate, the day you played God you hung an innocent man. I read the Marshal's report; Owen left Bisbee, as he had left other towns, because of his wife's affair with another man. It had happened once too often and his contempt for her became intolerable so he began to plan to get rid of her. It was just a matter of waiting for an opportunity and one night it came.

"Sure, Tom was at the Owen camp that night of the murder. He and Harp had been drinking and they got off the main road and came upon the Owen wagon by pure chance. Their loud talk and drunken laughter brought Owen out, and it was then that he decided to kill his wife and blame it on Tom. After they rode off he dragged his wife down by the spring and strangled her. He'd noticed the white button missing off Tom's shirt and it was a simple matter to find a white button and place it in his wife's hand, knowing it would be the clincher when Tom came to trial. How does that make you feel, Almighty Judge?"

Jed listened in disbelief and felt a strange mixture of emotions. He was glad that Tom was alive, yet fearful of the outcome of his return to Buell. Just then he noticed a man crossing the street from Rosita's toward the saloon. He recognized Harp, the bounty hunter and gunhand. Lordgodalmighty! he thought. Three gunslingers in town, all bent on revenge! This will be a day!

At that moment, a solitary rider entered Buell's

dusty main street. He rode erect in the saddle, staring straight ahead, past Applegate's store and stopped at the foot of the bridge. He sat there for a long moment or two, staring at the bridge before he stepped down to the street. Tom Pender had returned to Buell.

Johnny Stryker had seen Tom ride by and now he said to Jed, "Trot on out of here and tell the good people of this town that Tom Pender is back and he'll probably be wanting to talk to them."

Jed slipped out the side door and headed for Doc's office with his incredible tale. He was halfway across the street when he glanced over his shoulder and saw Tom enter the China Girl.

Harp had joined Mort at the bar and was drinking a beer. Johnny reseated himself at the table and watched him make the long walk from the door to the bar. At about the halfway point, he stopped to exchange glances with his three friends, then he continued toward Frank, who was backed against the wall, bewildered. Tom approached within a couple of paces and said, "Hello, Frank."

The sound of his voice was like escaping air, hoarse and whistling. Frank raised his eyes to Tom's face and shrank even closer against the wall. "We buried you," he whispered. "We hung you and buried you!"

"That you sure did," rasped Tom. "In fact, that's sorta what I'm here to see you about."

Johnny Stryker walked to Tom's side and took up the conversation. "It pains Tom some to talk," he said, "so let me tell you the plan. Tom here doesn't relish shooting anyone down in cold blood, not even you, Mister Applegate, but neither can he let this score go unsettled. You'd have to agree with that, now, wouldn't you, Mister Applegate?" Without waiting for an answer, he continued. "So, we're going to reenact that little trial you conducted a few months back and we're going to hold it in the exact same spot. Only this time, we'll be using guns instead of words. Everything will be fair and square; Mort, Harp and I are here to see that it is. And after you have been 'tried', Frank, each of the jury will have his turn. Since you were the judge, we thought it was only right that you be give the honor of being first. So, go strap on a gun, Mister Applegate and meet us out by the bridge."

Frank stood, staring at them, unable to move. Johnny waited a few seconds, then drew his gun and blasted a hole in the wall just a few inches from Frank's head.

"Mister Applegate, I don't have the principles Tom does. We're here to settle this thing and settle it we will. You have my word for it; if you give us any trouble, I'll give you a third eye right in the center of your forehead. Now move! Get a gun strapped on, get back here and be quick about it!"

Frank started for the side door, but Tom stopped him. "Just a minute," he said. He dug a nickel out of his pocket and tossed it toward Frank. "Brink me back a sack of licorice drops."

Jed had talked to Doc, Henry and Dolph, and the unbelievable story of the return of Tom Pender ran up and down Main Street with its own momentum. Soon a group had gathered in front of Holly's boarding house across the street from the China Girl Saloon.

The door of the saloon opened and Johnny stepped out to the boardwalk, followed by Mort, then Harp, and finally Tom. They stood four abreast for a few seconds, then Tom stepped into the center of the street, in case there were any doubts that he had returned. Johnny walked over to the crowd and explained the plan to them. Finally, Tom turned and walked toward the bridge and his three friends followed. The crowd moved on, keeping to the sidewalk until they were in front of Doc's office.

Johnny noticed that the men wore guns and a couple, including Henry carried shotguns. Tom stood in the heat of the sun and waited for Frank. Johnny had almost decided to go in after him when he saw the door of the store open and Frank emerged. He noted with satisfaction that Frank was wearing a gun.

Frank stopped at the foot of the steps. "Tom, you know I haven't got a chance against you. This is plain out murder. Can't we settle this some other way?" he pleaded.

"There's no other way," Johnny answered. "It's either me or Tom and at least Tom is giving you a chance--I told you it was to be fair and square. You know Tom's a leftie, so to even things up, he;s going to make his draw with his right hand.

"Another thing that might spur you on, Mister Applegate, you'll be fighting for the lives of all these other men because if you get Tom then Mort and Harp and I will ride out. It's his fight all the way; we're just here to enforce the rules. Of course, Tom's sort of planning on riding out of here with us, with your debt to him paid in full."

Frank looked at the faces of the townspeople, then looked back at Johnny and with an air of resignation, walked to the center of the street and turned to face Tom. The shadow on the canyon wall had crept halfway across Main Street. The two men stood, half in the shadow, half out.

"It seems this must be," said Frank with a heavy sigh, "but whichever way it goes, I want you to know I'm sorry for what happened, Tom."

"You forgot the licorice, Frank," Tom said and smiled.

Frank went for his gun, but even as he drew he knew he would be too late. Tom made a right-handed draw as fast as the flick of a bullwhip, tossing the gun to his left hand before he fired. It happened so fast that most of those looking on didn't see it.

Frank died with a bullet in his heart. The slug from Frank's gun dug into the ground at Tom's feet. Tom walked to Frank's side and stood over him a moment, then as he squatted down to examine the wound a blast from Henry's shotgun passed over his head and tore into the stomach of Mort Middleton. Mort let out a groan and sank to the street.

Before Mort hit the ground, Johnny Stryker's gun was in his hand. Harp had also drawn and was in a crouch. Johnny's first shot caught Henry full in the chest. He coughed blood, but kept his feet and lifted the shotgun to his shoulder, when Johnny's second shot found its mark and he dropped. Most of the townspeople scattered, but those who had served on the jury knew they had to fight it out. They were firing shot for shot with the gunmen, but they fired from panic and their aim was off. Many of them fell that day in the hot, dusty street of Buell.

Emory Miller emptied his gun at Johnny Stryker and one of the bullets found a vital spot. Johnny's knees buckled and he fell forward on his face and lay motionless. A second later Harp dropped Emory.

Tom was searching the crowd for jurymen when his eyes fastened on Jed. He leveled his gun to fire, but the memory of his one-time friendship with Jed caused him to hesitate a fraction of a second, and that hesitation cost him his life. Dolph Edelblut took advantage of Tom's diverted attention to raise his rifle, aim and fire. The high-powered slug knocked Tom off his feet and he landed on his back with blood soaking his shirt front.

When Tom fell, the firing stopped and the roar of the ensuing silence was louder than any noise. Five men lay dead and Tom Pender was dying. Harp squatted beside him.

"Sure looks like it was meant for me to cash in my stack in Buell," the dying man said.

Jed and Doc walked over and Doc started to examine the wound.

"Never mind, Doc," said Tom. "You ain't got a plug big enough for the hole that's in me." He looked up at Jed and motioned him closer. "Cut enough outta that twenty dollars you're holding' for me to buy Asa and Dolph a drink and tell 'em it's on Tom." He rolled his head toward Harp and gasped, "Would you build your ol' buddy a smoke?"

While Harp worked with paper and tobacco, Tom's eyes closed and his body relaxed. Jed and Doc realized they had just witnessed the second death of Tom Pender.

CHAPTER SEVENTEEN
Wooden Guns and Rose Bushes

As the weeks went by, the cataclysmic effect of the shootout on Main Street was profound. That changes were taking place was obvious. Wounds, old and new, mental and physical, were healing. People greeted each other with a touch of neighborliness. The death of six men, three of them Buell businessmen, became the bond that drew the rest of the town toward maturity.

Opal Applegate seemed to gain strength from the tragedy and carried on her husband's business with a surprising display of administrative genius. One of the teamsters from the mine took over Henry's livery stable.

Harp stayed on in Buell. He attended the funerals and paid his respects to friend and foe alike. He arranged for a room at Holly's and spent most of his time at the poker tables or the bar. At sometime during each evening he would say to Jed, "Guess I'll be pulling out tomorrow." But he never did.

After the shooting, the sale of the China Girl fell through and Jed resigned himself to tending bar yet a while longer.

Strange things happened as the Old West adjusted to the tumultuous times, one of them occurring following a town meeting at the schoolhouse; Harp, the bounty hunter, was asked to be the first marshal of Buell. He accepted the offer and became one of the outstanding lawmen in the Arizona Territory.

One afternoon shortly after he pinned on his badge he was talking to Doc in front of the China Girl when a stranger rode into town. Harp recognized the breed from a hundred feet away as a gunslinger on the prod. He stepped to the hitching rail and waited for the rider to approach. The man reined his horse to a stop and looked down at him.

"I hear you got a fast gun here goes by the name of Tom Pender."

"Well, I reckon there's no argument there," said Harp. "Tom's here, all right."

"Beins' I was a friend of Will Storms, I'd kinda like to talk to him. Know where I can find him?"

Harp walked closer and looked up at the man. "I reckon I do. You follow that path alongside Doc's office and you'll come to a cemetery. Tom's lying in the third grave from the gate."

In the next instant, Harp had his gun out and bout two inches of the barrel buried in the man's belly. "Hand me your gun real careful-like," he said. When he had the man's weapon, he prodded the barrel in a little deeper; then, with the universal authority of lawmen, he said, "Now you listen to me, Mister, and you listen real careful. You turn this nag around and ride outta here and stay out! There'll be no more gunslingers in Buell. We got law here now and I'm it! My name is Harp and don't you forget it. And tell those other vermin you crawl around with to stay outta Buell. Now, git!"

The man rode off considerably faster than he had ridden in. Harp watched him go, then squared his hat and turned back to Doc. Doc had a big smile on his face. "What you grinnin' at?" he said.

"That was a mighty fine job, Marshal. I'm thinking Buell just might get to be a good place to live in after all." He turned and headed toward his office. The sound of the school bell ringing for noon recess was music to his ears and for the first time in many years, he felt totally at peace.

"Hey, Doc," Harp called. "Join me in a beer?"

"Not right now," Doc answered. "I've got a little job I've been putting off too long. Got to give some care to Mary's rosebush; needs watering and some pruning." He continued toward his office and Harp disappeared into the China Girl. The sun-scorched September afternoon wore one.

A sparrow took a dust bath at the foot of the old bridge and through the silence that had settled on the town, the squeaking of an ore car coming out of Jefferson Buell's mine could be heard. The early afternoon shadows inched out from the base of the canyon and started crawling toward the town. The school bell rang, dismissing class for the day. Two small boys, playing on their way home, faced each other on the road. One pulled a wooden gun from his belt and pointed it at the other. "Bang! Bang! You're dead!" he said.

The "slain" one obediently fell to the road and lay still. His "slayer" replaced the gun in his belt and strutted toward home.

The Marshal left the China Girl and walked toward his office. He paused at the door and looked protectively over his town. Glancing at the thermometer by the door, he muttered, "Hotter'n the hinges of Hell!" and went inside, leaving the town to the silence and the sun.

THE END

COPIES OF THIS BOOK MAY BE ORDERED BY SENDING $6.95, PLUS $2.00 SHIPPING AND HANDLING TO:

LONGANHILL PRESS,
Box 1160,
Patagonia, Arizona,
85624

ARIZONA RESIDENTS ADD FIVE PERCENT (45 CENTS FOR SALES TAX.)